For Gabe, Matthew, and Luke,
my own swashbuckling heroes
—M.R.

DISNEP
PIRATES *of the* CARIBBEAN
DEAD MEN TELL NO TALES

The
BRIGHTEST STAR
in the
NORTH

The Adventures of
CARINA SMYTH

By MEREDITH RUSU

Based on Walt Disney's PIRATES OF THE CARIBBEAN
Based on Characters Created by TED ELLIOTT & TERRY ROSSIO
and STUART BEATTIE and JAY WOLPERT
Written by JEFF NATHANSON

DISNEP PRESS
LOS ANGELES · NEW YORK

Printed in the United States of America
First Hardcover Edition, April 2017
1 3 5 7 9 10 8 6 4 2
FAC-020093-17055

Library of Congress Control Number: 2016958412

ISBN 978-1-4847-8720-5

Designed by Gegham Vardanyan

disneybooks.com
disney.com/pirates

SUSTAINABLE FORESTRY INITIATIVE   Certified Sourcing
www.sfiprogram.org
SFI-00993

THIS LABEL APPLIES TO TEXT STOCK

PROLOGUE

THE MOON GLOWED WHITE IN THE NIGHT SKY, dipping in and out of sight among long clouds. The ground was eerily dark below. As each cloud passed, a shaft of moonlight illuminated shadowy forms outside the house. Swaying palm branches. A worn, frayed rope drooped low between two poles. And a post marking the entrance to the children's home.

There was no sign on the post. No welcome or even an indication that the home was special. People who needed it knew what it was, though most arrivals remained anonymous. It was better that way.

Far on the horizon, the clouds thickened. A storm was

brewing. It wouldn't reach the home for quite a while yet, but it would find its way. That was how it was on the islands—hints of frightening weather always lingering at the edges of the sea, bringing strong gales and torrents of rain that ripped across the land only to be replaced a short while later by calm skies. The half-hidden moon, the distant rumble of thunder, and the quickening breeze were all a matter of course. Even the shadows dancing around the orphanage were ordinary.

Only one shadow was out of place.

A man in a heavy coat—far too heavy for the island heat—hobbled toward the door. His arms were strong, but his weight was thrown off-balance by the basket in his hands. He clearly wanted to remain unseen. A beam of moonlight broke through the clouds and shone on the distinguished feather adorning his hat.

The man raised his coat collar a little higher and hobbled more quickly.

Good, he thought once he reached the steps of the children's home. *No one in sight.*

He gently placed the basket on the stairs and then lifted the blanket to peek inside. The child—an infant girl—was still asleep. *I wonder,* he thought. *Do all children sleep so soundly?*

He watched the infant for a long moment. Then the breeze picked up, and he replaced the blanket safely over her. He pulled a large book from his satchel and tucked it alongside the baby with a note. Short and to the point:

Her mother died. Her name is Carina Smyth.

An unusually large jewel crested the cover of the book. It caught the moon's light and reflected it—bloodred. A ruby.

It wasn't much. But it was all he could give the child.

"May the stars guide you," the man whispered. "Better than I could. Stay safe. And remember your namesake, the star that will always lead you home."

The man looked up. Through a break in the clouds, he could just make it out.

"Carina. The brightest star in the north."

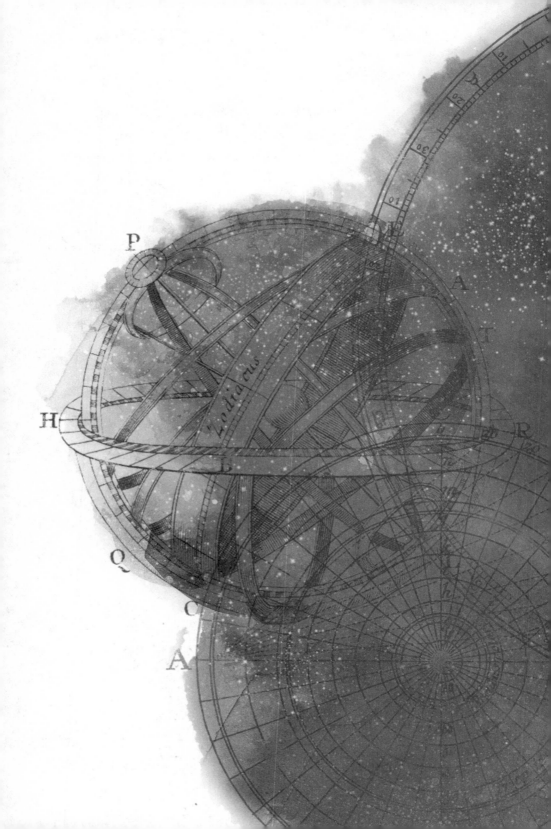

PART ONE
THE ORPHAN'S TOKEN

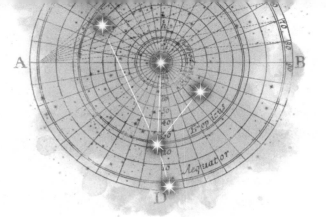

CHAPTER 1

"JUST STAY CLOSE, AND NO ONE WILL SEE US."

The girl and her companion crept up to the house through the tall grass. It was a small building, only one level with windows peeking into several tiny rooms. The wood on the outside was weathered and worn.

"We shouldn't be doing this," the young boy with her whispered nervously.

They helped each other up onto a crate so they could peer over a windowsill. Through the cracked glass, they spotted their target—the treasure—resting on a wooden table.

"We *really* shouldn't be doing this," the boy repeated.

"You said you didn't deserve to have it taken away."

Eight-year-old Carina Smyth shot him a look with her piercing blue eyes. "Were you telling the truth?"

"Of course," the boy, James, replied.

"Then you deserve to get it back," Carina said matter-of-factly. "If it was taken unjustly, you must have justice."

"But what if we get caught?" James whined. "I don't want to get whipped again."

"We won't get caught." Carina turned her attention to the treasure and smiled. *Not as long as you're with me,* she thought.

Quietly, the children raised the window. Carina jammed a stick into place to keep it from shutting. Then they slipped inside.

The room was dark but only slightly cooler than outside. It was an unusually hot day for that part of the country. Carina liked that.

She'd been at many children's homes in her young life and had seen all sorts of weather: rain, sleet, drought, and snow. Her curious nature and sharp tongue always landed her in trouble: the kind that prompted benefactors to pack her bags and send her to be someone else's problem. She'd been at her current home the longest, and the owner was a kindly old man named Lord Willoughby. Carina had never met him. But all the keepers said he was extremely benevolent, and it was because of his charity that they put up with "ill-mannered orphans" like her.

Deep in the English countryside, the weather usually consisted of rain, rain, and more rain. Yet there were those rare occasions, like that day, when it reached that perfect combination of sun that was just hot enough to warm your hair and dampen your hands and a passing breeze that cooled you off before either became too bothersome. In Carina's opinion, that was how every day should be.

Now she focused all her attention on the treasure: a small bag of marbles on the table corner.

The floorboards creaked under her and James's feet as they moved. James hesitated.

"It's okay," Carina whispered. "Come on."

Swiftly, she led James across the room. They didn't have long, but Carina was certain her plan would work. From her shift pocket, she pulled out a small bag identical to the one on the table. It was lumpy and the contents tumbled in her palm. Unlike the treasure bag of marbles, her bag was filled with small stones.

Quickly, Carina scooped up the marbles and replaced them with the dummy bag of stones. She handed the treasure to James. "Justice," she said with a wink.

That was when they heard it: footsteps outside the door.

"Go!" Carina whispered urgently.

She and James stole across the floor. Without hesitating, she gave him a lift using her hands as an impromptu step so he could hop up and over the windowsill. She was just about to jump through the window herself when—

"Who's in there? What's going on?"

The door to the room opened. There was no time!

In one swift motion, Carina yanked the stick from the sill, and the window slammed.

"Carina!" She could hear James's muffled cry through the glass. But she stayed calm as the adults entered the room.

"Miss Smyth? What in heaven's name do you think you are doing?" a man with a crooked nose and angry eyes demanded. He and a woman in plain attire entered the room.

"It is very hot today, Mr. Conway," Carina replied innocently. "I wanted to cool off."

"In the keepers' quarters?" he said accusingly. The home's secretary, Mr. Conway liked to be involved with more than matters of finance. He often patrolled the halls, making sure things were running to his liking. "You are not permitted to be in this room." A knowing look flashed across his face. He barreled over to the table and grabbed the bag of stones.

Carina held her breath.

Mr. Conway bounced the bag in his hand. The weight of the stones was enough to fool him. He mistook it for the bag of marbles. With a huff, he tossed it back to the table.

Carina couldn't help smiling a little.

"Do you think this is a game, girl?" the man asked crossly.

"No, sir," Carina replied. "The keepers don't allow us to play games in the heat, for risk of exhaustion."

"I was not speaking of the keepers," Mr. Conway said.

"But you spoke of games," Carina replied.

"The game you appear to think this is," he said.

"But I am not playing a game," Carina said. "The keepers don't allow it."

"Impertinent girl!" Mr. Conway snapped. "The whip will wipe that smile from your face."

"Mr. Conway," the woman in plain clothing spoke gently. Her name was Mrs. Altwood; she was one of the main guardians—or keepers—at the orphanage. "You cannot blame the child for trying to escape the heat. Even the livestock will not leave the barn today."

"Discomfort is no excuse," he said. "She must learn discipline."

"I'm sure Carina won't do it again." Mrs. Altwood looked at Carina meaningfully. "And that she will mind the quarters which are off limits more carefully. Isn't that right, child?"

"Yes, ma'am." Carina nodded.

Mrs. Altwood walked to the table and gently touched the bag of stones. Her face grew serious. "If you are uncomfortable, perhaps it would be cooler by the creek, where the women are washing clothes. I will lead you there to assist them."

Carina resisted pulling a face. She *hated* washing clothes. The smell of lye stuck to her hands for days. And the water used to wash the clothes was boiling. It was definitely *not* cooler by the creek. But Carina had a feeling Mrs. Altwood knew about that, as well as about the marbles.

"Yes, ma'am," Carina said through tight lips. "Thank you, ma'am."

Mrs. Altwood smiled. "Come, child. There are clothes to be washed."

* * *

"He was not at fault," Carina insisted as Mrs. Altwood pulled her along over the field toward the creek. "The other boys stole his marbles and teased him at breakfast. James did not deserve to have them taken away."

"And I will speak to the other boys," said Mrs. Altwood. "But you must not keep getting into mischief. And above all you *must* learn to hold your tongue. There are far more powerful men in the world than Mr. Conway. Cross them and you could end up in prison. A young lady must learn her place."

Carina yanked her arm away from Mrs. Altwood. "I am not a young lady," she huffed. "I'm an orphan."

Mrs. Altwood sighed. "Even orphans can turn into the most well-mannered young ladies. But if you do not learn to curb that tongue, then the only way to knock some sense into you will be with the whip."

They had reached the creek. Village women and some of

the older girls from the children's home were already hard at work, scrubbing and beating dirty laundry clean.

"I was just standing up for James," Carina insisted. "The boys mocked him, stole his token, and then the keepers took it away. He was wronged by everyone. Where is the justice in that?"

"Everyone will face justice in their own time." Mrs. Altwood placed her hands firmly on Carina's shoulders. "But that is not your responsibility. Your responsibility is to stay out of trouble and grow into the young lady your father wanted you to become. Do you understand?"

Hearing mention of her father gave Carina pause. Mrs. Altwood was the only keeper who knew how much the man who had left Carina on the steps of a distant orphanage years before meant to her. Carina pouted, but she nodded.

"Good," said Mrs. Altwood. "Now take hold of a washboard and start scrubbing."

Carina stomped off, grabbing a washboard along the way.

"Quite the devil's tongue in that girl." A lady holding linens walked up to Mrs. Altwood. "She could do with a good lashing."

Mrs. Altwood nodded. "Perhaps. But her heart is in the right place. I believe it's better to direct a fire than snuff it out." She nodded at the flames burning under a pot of boiling clothes. "So that one day, it will grow to be useful."

"Unless it burns you first," the woman noted.

Mrs. Altwood chuckled. "Of that I am certain. If there's one thing I know about Carina Smyth, it's that her personality burns as brightly as a star."

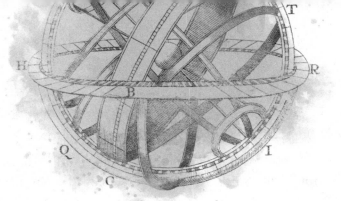

CHAPTER 2

"DID YOU GET IN A LOT OF TROUBLE?" James whispered that night.

He, Carina, and their friend Sarah all sat in their favorite meeting spot: under a large tree at the edge of the fields surrounding the children's home. Naturally, the children weren't allowed out of the house after hours. But the three friends had figured out ways to slip out unseen.

"Not too much trouble." Carina leaned back. "Mr. Conway wanted to whip me, but Mrs. Altwood made me wash laundry instead." She stuck out her tongue. "I think I would have preferred whipping."

Sarah snickered. "Of course Miss Carina Smyth would prefer the punishment of a hero to that of a servant."

Sarah was older than Carina and James by three years and had been at that children's home her whole life. Being older meant she tended to put Carina in her place.

"It's not that," said Carina. "But I *hate* the smell of lye, and Mrs. Altwood knows it."

"I'm sorry you got caught because of me," James moaned. "I told you we would get in trouble."

Carina shrugged. "It wasn't that bad. And you needed your token back. It's important."

James spilled the marbles out from the pouch into his palm. Ten smooth spheres, carved from different shades of wood.

James and Carina were two of the lucky orphans to have been left with tokens, or special objects that identified them if their parents ever decided to return. There weren't many children at that home—about twenty in all. Carina had heard stories of larger homes closer to London, but those were workhouses. Out in the country, it was easy to feel like the world had forgotten about them. Like time was passing on while they stayed, waiting for someone—anyone—to come and collect them.

"Maybe my father is a carpenter," James said thoughtfully. "He'd need to be skilled to make these."

"*He* probably didn't make them," Sarah pointed out.

Carina gave Sarah a look. "That's not fair. You don't know that. You should be nicer."

"Easy to say when you have a token," Sarah said, a bit bitterly. "My parents didn't leave me anything."

"Maybe they died," said Carina. "That's what's happened to me. My mother died, so my father left me on the steps of a children's home."

"But at least he left you a token." Sarah pointed to the book in Carina's hands.

The three friends gazed down at the cover. The ruby cresting the front twinkled in the starlight.

"You really don't remember where he left you?" James asked.

"Should I remember being born?" Carina giggled. "No. I've been in lots of homes. But no one ever knew where I came from."

"What do you remember?" asked Sarah.

A faraway look crossed Carina's face. "Bits and pieces. Other children in other homes. Traveling on ships. And a song. Something about guiding or light." Carina looked down at the book in her hands. "Every now and then I have a dream of being told to hold on to this. That my father meant for me to have it. That it is my birthright."

"Can you read it?" asked James.

Carina shook her head. "Mrs. Altwood says it's in Italian. I think it talks about the stars." She flipped the book open to several pages in the center filled with astronomical diagrams. To the children, the charts looked like intricate spiderwebs dotted with little bursts of penned light.

"I just need to find someone to teach me Italian," Carina said, determined. "Or learn it myself."

"You could sell the book," Sarah commented. "That ruby must be worth a fortune. Any family in the village would be happy to take you in if it meant they'd get that."

Carina shook her head vehemently. "No, I'm never giving it up. My father meant for me to have it. There must be something important in it that he wanted me to know."

Suddenly, a branch snapped in the darkness. The friends looked up, alert.

"If one of the keepers finds us, we'll all be whipped," whispered James.

"It's probably just a rabbit," said Sarah. She stared into the shadows of the surrounding fields. "I don't see anyone."

"Then let's head back," said James. "I've had enough close calls for one day."

The friends quietly slipped away from the tree and went back to the room where all the children slept.

None of them noticed the curious eyes watching them from the shadows.

CHAPTER 3

"TUTTE LE VERITÀ SARANNO COMPRESE QUANDO le stesse si saranno derectus."

Carina mouthed the words slowly to herself. She was lying in her bed, studying the book her father had left her. All the children were in the common quarters on their sleeping cots.

Carina traced the letters on the page. There wasn't much written in the book that she could understand. The keepers had taught the children in the home how to read English, but Italian was completely foreign to her. And it wasn't as though she could ask them for help learning it. Mrs. Altwood was the only keeper in the home who knew about Carina's token, and the old woman had instructed Carina to keep the book out of sight. It was very unusual for a child to have such a valuable-looking book, let alone one with a ruby on the cover.

"Le stelle si derectus," Carina repeated. Even if she didn't understand it, she was determined to *read* it. That way, whenever she did learn Italian, she would know every word by heart.

I wonder, did my father read these very words? She ran her finger along the misaligned scribbles. *Maybe he is still alive, searching for me. He must be a very wise man. Not many people would leave their child a book with charts of the stars. Maybe he's a scientist.*

Carina turned the pages delicately, as if they were made from pressed flower petals. She stopped when she reached the very first page in the book. A name was inscribed in bold ink:

GALILEO GALILEI

Galileo Galilei wasn't her father; she knew that much. Her last name was Smyth. But whenever she asked the keepers about Galileo Galilei, they either shook their heads or brushed her aside, telling her to mind the matters of a properly behaved young woman.

Yet tucked in the back of Carina's memory alongside the wispy recollections of ships and a song, Carina had an inkling that Galileo Galilei was a man of science.

"Galileo Galilei," she whispered to herself. "That sounds like the name of a scholar."

A stern voice rang out across the room. "Look sharp!"

Instantly, all the children snapped to attention.

Mr. Conway strode into the room, followed by two keepers. As quick as a rabbit, Carina slipped the book in her pillowcase.

He looked down his nose at the children.

"It has come to my attention that there are stolen items here at the home," he said.

The children all murmured in concern. That made Mr. Conway smile.

"Items which have been stolen by the wards here," he continued. "Your belongings will be searched. Anyone discovered with stolen valuables will be severely punished."

The keepers began dumping all the children's meager possessions into the center of the room. There wasn't much. A corncob doll. A woven blanket. Some spare clothing and toy hoops.

Meanwhile, the children looked at one another in fear. Stealing was punishable by whipping, or even being sent to the workhouses. Carina could see the other children racking their brains, trying to remember if there was anything in their belongings they shouldn't have.

The keepers reached James's bed and flipped the frame

over. Carina gulped. James's token satchel fell open, and a cascade of marbles spilled onto the floor. But Mr. Conway didn't seem to notice. None of the keepers did. In fact, Carina had a feeling Mr. Conway's eyes were on her the whole time.

The keepers reached her bed next. They flipped it over, spilling her lumpy pillow, spare shift, and prized book on the floor.

"Well, well, what have we here?" Mr. Conway stepped forward. In one swift motion, he snatched the book from the floor. "A rare and valuable tome such as this surely couldn't belong to an orphan girl, could it, Miss Smyth?"

"That is my token!" Carina cried, lunging forward. The keepers held her back, gripping her arms tightly enough to leave marks. "It was left with me as an infant, by my father."

Mr. Conway tsked. "Come now, child, you'll need a better story than that to save you from the whip. Even your friends know that story is a lie."

Mr. Conway glanced in Sarah's direction. The girl flushed and lowered her head.

"Sarah?" Carina's voice caught.

James spoke up. "She's not lying. Carina has had that book her whole life."

"Perhaps you would like to join your friend in punishment?" Mr. Conway's eyes flashed in James's direction.

Rustling skirts suddenly whooshed through the door.

"What is going on here?" Mrs. Altwood demanded. "What has happened to the children?"

"What has happened," Mr. Conway said, placing Carina's book securely in his jacket, "is that we have discovered a thief in our midst."

"He took my token!" Carina cried desperately. The keepers still held her back, and her arms began to prickle with pins and needles.

"Mr. Conway, I can attest that the child has had that book ever since she arrived," Mrs. Altwood said. "Ever since she was born. She is not lying—it was left to her by her father. It said as much in the letter from the keepers of her previous home."

"Then her father must have stolen it," Mr. Conway snapped. "What abandoned water rat is left with such a valuable item?"

"My father left it for me to learn from, to study!" Carina blurted out. "It is by Galileo Galilei, a man of science."

The secretary slowly turned his head in Carina's direction. "Careful, girl. Or there will be more than just the whip in your future."

But Carina was furious. "You accuse me of stealing, but it is *you* who are the thief!"

"Enough!" Mr. Conway's voice made the children shudder. "Bring her to my study. I will personally make sure she answers for her crime."

The keepers shoved Carina toward the door. Meanwhile, Mrs. Altwood hurried out of the room with the same rustle of skirts with which she had arrived.

Carina shot one last look at Sarah, whose head still hung low, before the door to the common quarters slammed.

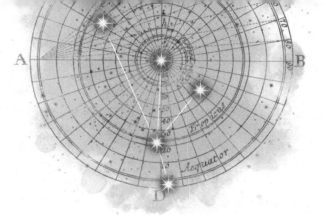

CHAPTER 4

THE CLOCK IN THE CORNER of Mr. Conway's study ticked by the seconds with striking severity. Carina stared hard at the secretary. He sat at his desk, tapping his fingers on the cover of the book in time with the clock.

"Tell me, child," he said. "If your father owned this, then where did he obtain it?"

"I do not know, sir," Carina said through gritted teeth.

"You don't know?" the man asked. "But you were so *certain* it was not stolen."

"It was not stolen by me," Carina replied. "My father passed it to me as my birthright. It was clearly his intention for me to study it."

A smile played across Mr. Conway's lips. "Was your father"—he read the opening page of the book—"'Galileo Galilei'?"

Carina shook her head. "My last name is Smyth."

"Are you aware, Miss Smyth, of who Galileo Galilei is?"

Carina paused. "He is a man of science."

"*Was* a man of science." The secretary closed the book, allowing the ruby to catch the light from the window. "And science is forbidden for a girl to study. The content of this diary is strictly for men. Should you pursue it any further, you will be taken for a witch."

Carina caught her breath. "It is a diary?"

Mr. Conway's smile turned to a sneer. "I tell you that you are in danger of being branded a witch, a crime punishable by death, and your main concern is that this book is a *diary*?"

Carina didn't reply.

"I am doing you a favor, Miss Smyth," Mr. Conway said. "Forget this book and we shall let the entire incident pass."

At that, Carina's temper flared. "I am not leaving without my token! It is my birthright. You wish to steal it because of the ruby!"

Carina had never seen the man's eyes flash so viciously. She knew she was in great danger. But nothing else mattered to her now—only the book.

"I daresay the gallows certainly are in your future," the secretary said, his voice low and menacing. "But I am a fair man. I will give you a chance to *earn* this token back."

Mr. Conway flipped the book open to a random page.

"Read the words on this page, and I will return the book to you," he said.

Carina breathed shallowly as she stepped forward. She looked down at the page Mr. Conway had opened to, her heart pounding.

And then she smiled.

"*'Tutte le verità saranno comprese quando le stesse si saranno derectus,'*" she read smoothly, happy all her practice had come in handy.

Mr. Conway's face flushed red with anger.

"Demon child! Where did you learn to read that?"

"I have read the words correctly," Carina said, triumphant. "Return my token."

"I will return nothing," Mr. Conway spat. "You have only proven yourself to be in the devil's service. No child would know how to speak this language, let alone read it."

Carina was ready to explode. "You must keep your promise!" she exclaimed. "*Tutte le verità saranno comprese quando le stesse si saranno derectus! Tutte le verità saranno comprese quando le stesse si saranno derectus!* It means . . . well, it says—"

"All truths will be understood once the stars align."

Carina and Mr. Conway whirled toward the new voice. In the doorway stood Mrs. Altwood with a man in stately attire whom Carina had never seen before.

"Lord Willoughby." Mr. Conway stood at attention. "I was not expecting your arrival."

"I asked him to come," Mrs. Altwood said, "as the benefactor of this home."

The man strode into the room. "I hear there has been a disruption," he said. "That a child has been accused of theft."

Mr. Conway nodded. "Unfortunately, yes, my lord. This child was found in possession of a valuable book. Surely no orphan would ever possess such a treasure without theft."

Lord Willoughby picked up the book and examined it. "Yes, it is quite a treasure," he remarked. "I'm sure some would see it only for the gem on its cover."

Mr. Conway wilted under Lord Willoughby's stare.

"I—I cannot say, my lord," he stammered. "But surely it cannot remain with the child."

"It is my birthright!" Carina shouted. Mrs. Altwood shot her a warning look, and Carina softened her tone. "Left to me by my father, as my token."

Lord Willoughby nodded. "A token such as this speaks of great love. Far be it from us to separate a child from the only item she has left from her father. Wouldn't you agree, Mr. Conway?"

The man sputtered. "I—but, my lord—"

"I believe there are words between us far overdue." Lord Willoughby spoke to the secretary, but his eyes never left the book. "You will wait for me outside, Mr. Conway, and we will ride to my mansion to discuss your continued patronage of this home."

The secretary's face paled. "Of course, my lord," he said.

Mr. Conway glared at Carina venomously before leaving the room. Once the door had closed, Lord Willoughby turned to Carina.

"Is this book indeed your token?" he asked.

"Yes, sir," Carina said, tears beginning to fall. "My father meant for me to have it. Mrs. Altwood told me to keep it hidden."

The man handed her the book. "Then you must do as Mrs. Altwood says. Unless you keep it out of sight, it will attract more unwanted attention. Do you understand?"

Carina nodded.

Lord Willoughby noticed how tightly she clutched the book.

"Do you speak Italian?" he asked gently.

Carina shook her head. "No, sir. I do not."

"But I heard you recite the words when Mr. Conway asked," Lord Willoughby replied. *"Tutte le verità saranno comprese quando le stesse si saranno derectus."*

"I have been *trying* to read them," Carina admitted. "And sounding them out as best I could."

"I see." The man thought for a long moment. "Mr. Conway is right about one thing, at least: it is not becoming of a young lady to dabble in science."

Lord Willoughby looked at Mrs. Altwood. "There is nothing else known about her father?"

"I'm afraid not," Mrs. Altwood replied. "The child has no one."

"And yet, he left her this," Lord Willoughby said. "Very strange indeed." He contemplated quietly to himself. "I suppose . . . the study of language is not unheard of for a girl. In fact, it can be of great value. Tell me, Carina, do you wish to learn Italian?"

Carina's eyes shone. She nodded vehemently, too emotional to speak. She had always heard of Lord Willoughby's generosity but had had no idea it extended that far.

The man smiled. "Then so you shall. Mrs. Altwood and I will see to that."

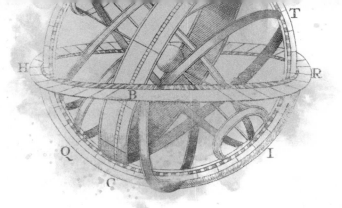

CHAPTER 5

"WHAT DO YOU THINK?" James asked curiously.

Carina grinned. "I think we should do it."

The children reread the sign posted on the town store.

COME ONE, COME ALL!

FESTIVAL AND REVELRY

GAMES, DELIGHTS, AND MYSTERIES FROM AFAR!

It was summertime. Nearly a year had passed since the incident with Mr. Conway. Carina and James had been sent along with other children from the home to purchase trinkets for the upcoming wedding of Miss Esther, one of the keepers' friends.

"The sign says it's this weekend," said Carina excitedly. "The keepers won't even notice we're missing. They're all too busy with the wedding preparations. And Mrs. Altwood is away until the end of the month, visiting her sister. We can sneak out and return home before sunset. They'll never know we were away."

"What are you two talking about?"

Sarah came up behind them, carrying an armful of ribbons and buttons.

"Nothing to concern yourself with," Carina said brusquely. She turned and led James down the street.

Sarah groaned. "Are you ever going to forgive me, Carina?"

"For nearly costing me the one thing I care about most?" Carina clutched her satchel more tightly. The book had never left her side since the incident with Mr. Conway. "Highly unlikely."

"I told you," Sarah insisted, trying to keep up. "Mr. Conway forced me to tell him where it was. I didn't know he was going to take it."

"But you told him I stole it?" Carina whirled on Sarah. The girls had had the same argument many, many times before. "You were jealous that you didn't have a token, and you tried to have mine taken away," Carina said. "What's worse, I thought you were my friend. I will not make that mistake twice."

Sarah winced.

"Let's go," Carina said to James. "The keepers need these supplies. We don't want to arouse any other suspicions by staying away for too long."

* * *

The weekend of the festival arrived. Carina had been right: sneaking away from the children's home had been incredibly easy, thanks to all the commotion the keepers were making over Esther's wedding. Carina and James slipped out in the afternoon without so much as a second look from anyone.

"This is so exciting!" said James. "I've always wanted to see a festival."

"I want to know what 'mysteries from afar' the poster was talking about," Carina said, her eyes shining. "Maybe there will be craftsmen there from France, or even Italy!"

By habit, Carina reached down and patted Galileo's diary, safely tucked in her satchel. Lord Willoughby had kept his promise. Twice a week, Carina practiced Italian with a tutor all the way from London. It was an incredibly rare opportunity for a young girl, let alone an orphan. Carina had picked up the basics remarkably quickly; even the master noted that she was an exceptionally motivated student. Mrs. Altwood and Lord Willoughby had firmly instructed Carina to keep the lessons to herself, lest she draw envy from her peers. Carina had listened, for the most part. The only one who knew she had been taking the lessons was James.

"Can you read the book now?" James asked eagerly.

"It's hard," Carina admitted. "The master is patient with me. I can read from his lesson manual, but I'm having trouble reading Galileo's diary."

"I still can't believe you're learning Italian." James shook his head. "You must have been born under a lucky star to be so fortunate."

Carina smiled. "Actually, the master told me that I'm named after a constellation." Carina took Galileo's diary from her satchel and pointed to the symbol on the cover: a cluster of five stars with the ruby in the center. "Carina is the name of the brightest star in the north," she explained. "That's what my father named me after. He must have been an astronomer to do that."

"An astronomer?" James asked.

Carina nodded. "Someone who gains knowledge by studying the stars."

James hesitated. "You mean like . . . like a witch?"

"No, no." Carina shook her head. "The very opposite. Witches do not exist. But if they did, they would be practicing magic. Science is the opposite of magic. It is the study of truth."

James looked a little overwhelmed. "You frighten me sometimes when you speak. I do not know any other girl who talks the way you do. Of stars, and science, and magic."

Carina laughed. "But I do not speak of magic. Only science . . . and anything I have learned from the master. Well, what he has mentioned. He doesn't want me to focus on the contents of the diary. Only the language."

The friends had reached the village. A large field off the square center was decorated entirely for the festival. Carina and James gasped. They had never seen anything like it! Tents and poles with ribbons were arranged everywhere. Pens were filled with prized livestock. There were flowers. And *people*! Carina could not remember seeing so many people in one place at the same time. Men and women and children, all enjoying the music and revelry.

"This is incredible," Carina breathed. "Come, James!"

The friends ran forward, laughing. They inhaled the festival air, rich with the scents of ale and sugary treats. They watched as men competed in feats of strength, and several times they needed to scamper away as the competition turned into an all-out brawl. Carina marveled at women in fine clothes waving fans and young folks playing games of chance.

"I wish we could play a game," said James, longingly eyeing village children bobbing for apples.

"We will," said Carina. "If that's what you'd like to spend our coins on. But we only have a few. Let's see the whole festival before deciding."

She and James continued to wander through the thick crowds of villagers. It was easy to become lost in the excitement. For the first time in her life, Carina felt like she was more than just an orphan—like she was part of something larger.

Then she saw a brightly colored tent standing off to one side, separated from the rest of the festival. Strange plants adorned the opening. Carina had once seen a drawing of something similar on display in the village market. What were they called? Palm branches?

An abnormally short man with a monkey on his shoulder stood outside the tent, playing a strange instrument. It whistled and whined as he squeezed it back and forth.

Through the opening, Carina could see a woman sitting in the center of the tent. Before her was a table, draped in dark cloth and lit by a glowing candelabra. She wore a long, loose-fitting garment layered with different-colored materials. A twisted kerchief snaked around her head, and her dark curly hair spilled out beneath it. Her feet were bare.

Carina had never before seen people who dressed like that, had not known people who kept foreign animals and played strange music.

The woman at the center of the tent scanned the crowd. Her dark eyes rested on Carina.

James gulped. "Who do you think *they* are?" he asked.

"No idea." Carina shook her head.

Without thinking, Carina walked toward the tent.

"Carina!" James whispered loudly.

But she wasn't listening. She felt completely absorbed by the colors and the music and the swaying palm branches. As she reached the tent, the monkey danced around her feet.

"Come, child." The woman with the dark eyes smiled. "We've been expecting you."

CHAPTER 6

"THAT IS NOT POSSIBLE," Carina said in her normal self-assured voice. But it sounded strange to her, as though she were listening to herself say the words from a distance. "I do not know you."

"But I know you." The woman held out her hand. "I know everything."

"Carina!" James hurried up next to her and tugged her arm. "I don't like this."

But Carina held fast. "You cannot know everything," she stated. "Even scientists do not know everything."

"I do not speak of science," the woman replied. "I speak

of fortune. The mysteries of the islands. I can see all with my third eye. And you will see what I see . . . for a small offering."

"See?" insisted James. "She just wants your money. This is not what I want to spend our coins on. Let's go."

Carina still didn't budge. "There is no such thing as a third eye. You say you are offering knowledge. But science—the study of *truth*—is the only way to obtain knowledge."

The woman's smile widened. "Then, please, allow me to 'study' you. I can tell you all you need to know."

Carina couldn't explain why, but everything about the tent—the woman, the man, and the music, even the monkey—made her feel hot. Angry. Like she had a burning sensation in her chest she wanted to rip out. This woman was wrong. And Carina would prove it.

Carina opened her satchel and pulled out her coins.

"Don't!" said James.

But Carina slapped them on the table and sat down.

Silently, the woman passed her hand over the coins. Just like that, they were gone.

"Now, child," she said, "give me your hand."

Carina did as she was told. The woman studied Carina's palm. Carefully, she traced the lines with her long, tinted nails. Carina didn't like the feel of the woman's nails on her skin; they were gnarled and brittle.

"I see storms in your past," the woman spoke, her eyes

unfocused. "Dark clouds. A ship. The sea. You have traveled far for one so young."

Carina was about to ask from where, but she caught herself. The woman was making things up. She had to be.

The woman continued, tracing the longest line on Carina's palm. "Your quest for the truth will consume you," she said. "You will travel again, with the stars as your guide. The islands are calling you home."

"This is nonsense." Carina yanked her hand away. "I am not from the islands."

The woman's dark eyes focused again and met Carina's. "Are you sure?" she asked.

Carina started to speak, then closed her mouth. The truth was she wasn't sure.

"There is a fire burning in your heart," the woman said. "It will not cease until you have vanquished it, or it has consumed you. I can see it with my third eye. It burns bright red—like a ruby."

The woman's gaze drifted to Carina's satchel. Carina hadn't noticed that when she'd withdrawn the coins from her bag, the top had remained open. Galileo's diary stuck out, visible to all in the tent. The ruby glinted in the light of the candelabra.

"Treasure has a way of making itself known," the woman finished quietly.

Carina buckled her satchel shut and stood. "You have

spoken but I have learned nothing of the truth from your words. Only guesses as to what may be. The monkey could have told me as much."

The woman's eyes flashed, but she didn't respond.

"Carina, can we please go now?" James begged.

"Yes," Carina said shortly. "We are finished here."

Carina turned and followed James out of the tent. Then the young boy anxiously pulled her along into the crowds.

The short man stepped up to the woman with the dark hair. The monkey scrambled up his leg and onto his shoulder.

"Was that the treasure?" he asked quietly.

The woman nodded. "Yes," she said, smiling. "The map."

* * *

The sun dipped lower in the sky as Carina and James made their way home from the festival. James munched happily on a cone of sweet bread.

"Best three coins I ever spent," he said, mouth full.

Carina rolled her eyes. "The only three coins you ever spent."

"Still the best." James swallowed. "Do you want a bite?"

"No, thank you," Carina said. She clutched the satchel at her side.

"You've been acting strange ever since that woman told

your fortune." James licked his fingers. "I thought you said it wasn't real."

"It wasn't," Carina said. "I just didn't like the way she looked at me. Or the monkey."

"You didn't like the way the monkey looked at you?" asked James.

"No, just . . . all of it." Carina shuddered. "The woman, the music, the monkey—it was disturbing."

"Then why did you insist on having your fortune told?" asked James. "I warned you not to spend your money there."

Carina paused. "I don't know," she answered truthfully.

They continued along the path back to the children's home. The sky grew overcast above them. Gray clouds gathered.

"Rain is coming," said Carina. "We should take the shorter way through the woods."

She and James looked to the right. Thick trees marked the entrance to the forest. Not far beyond the perimeter was the creek. They could follow it all the way to the orphanage.

"I don't like going through the woods," James groaned. "The keepers say there are wild animals in there."

Carina scoffed. "They say that to scare you. To keep us from going there on our own."

"Then . . . shouldn't we *not* go there on our own?" asked James.

"We already are on our own," said Carina. "And it will be

worse for us if we get caught in the storm. We can make it back faster if we follow the creek. Come on."

Carina tugged James's arm, and together they headed into the forest.

"Do you think the keepers will have noticed we were gone?" James asked.

"For our own sakes, let's hope not," said Carina.

James grew unusually quiet as they walked. "Do you think anyone would notice if we were gone?"

"What do you mean?" Carina ducked under a low branch.

"It's just . . ." James paused. "At the festival today, I saw children. With mothers and fathers. Holding hands. Some even rode on their parents' shoulders. I think they would notice if their children were gone. The parents, I mean. But if we disappeared, do you think the keepers would look for us? Or would they just . . . forget?"

The late-afternoon light passing through the leaves played across Carina's set jaw.

"I think we should rely on ourselves," she said. "But for what it's worth, I would not forget you."

James nodded.

The pair remained quiet until they reached the creek.

"Here we are," said Carina. She wiped her damp brow. "Almost home."

Just then, a branch snapped loudly behind them.

Carina and James whirled around.

"It's an animal," James said, frightened.

"Or a person," said Carina. She raised her voice. "Whoever you are—show yourself!"

James and Carina watched the trees intently. There was a rustling sound from behind a large trunk.

"Who are you?" Carina demanded.

"I know we are no longer friends." The person stepped out of hiding. "But it's cruel to pretend you've forgotten me."

Carina breathed in sharply. "What are you doing here, Sarah?"

"I wanted to go to the festival, too," Sarah complained. "So I followed you."

"You followed us to the festival?" Carina said crossly.

"You were there the whole time?" James asked.

Sarah nodded. "Well, for most of it."

"Why didn't you just tell us you wanted to come?" asked James.

"Because neither of you will speak to me anymore!" exclaimed Sarah.

"And whose fault is that?" Carina said angrily. "If you want friends so badly, then why don't you befriend the other orphans?"

"Because *no one* will talk to me," Sarah said quietly. "Not since everyone thinks I turned you in to Mr. Conway. They're all afraid."

"And rightly so," said Carina. "That's exactly what you did."

"I swear, I didn't mean for you to get in trouble." Sarah started crying. "He asked me about the book. Said wasn't it strange that a father would abandon his daughter with a jewel? He asked how come I was never left with something so precious. Did I suppose my parents didn't love me? I didn't even mean to tell him where it was. I'm really, truly sorry."

Carina didn't respond. She hadn't ever heard that much of Sarah's confession. But then again, she hadn't really ever let her get that far.

"I can only stay at the children's home for a little while longer before they send me to be a servant somewhere." Sarah wiped her nose. "Can't I at least be with you again until then?"

James looked up at Carina. "I think she's really sorry," he said.

After a long moment, Carina huffed. "Ugh, come on, then. If we don't get back before dark, we will be missed."

Sarah scampered up to join them, and the three children trudged on.

It wasn't exactly like old times. But Carina noted that it did feel nice to have a companion on her left and right again.

The children reached a small bridge over the creek that they needed to cross. Suddenly, they stopped short.

"Oh, no, the bridge is out," said James. He pointed to

the splintered wood. Some jagged pieces were still floating away. "Now what do we do?"

Carina scanned the creek. "Maybe we can hop across on the rocks," she said. "It's not that deep."

Thunder rumbled ominously in the distance.

"Come on," she insisted. "Or we'll get caught in the storm."

"A storm may be coming," a voice growled behind them.

Carina, James, and Sarah all whipped around. Behind them stood the short man and the dark-haired woman from the festival tent—along with three more men.

The short man's eyes glinted. "But that's the least of your worries."

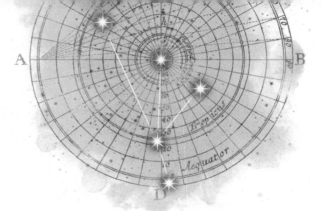

CHAPTER 7

"RUN!" EXCLAIMED CARINA.

The friends bolted, sprinting away from the creek and deeper into the woods. But they weren't fast enough to outrun the men. They grabbed Carina first.

"Let me go!" Carina cried as two of the rogues pinned her arms.

"Leave her alone!" yelled James. He picked up a nearby stick and swatted at one man's face.

"Yeow!" the man yelped. James had caught him in the eye.

Carina took advantage of the distraction and bit the hand of the second man who held her—hard.

The man cried out in pain and let go. In that split second, Carina darted away.

"Devil child!" he screamed. "You will pay for that." He reached out to grab her again, but a stone smacked him in the face.

It had come from Sarah. She had grabbed several rocks from the creek bed, held them in her skirt, and pelted the men with them.

"This way!" Sarah shouted. She motioned for James and Carina to follow her. Together, the children dove under a large fallen tree trunk and scampered through piles of broken brambles and branches.

The men and the dark-haired woman followed, but they were larger than the children. The forest debris made it more difficult to follow where the friends ran.

"We have to get back to the home," Carina said to Sarah and James. "If we get to the creek, we can make it there."

"But the bridge . . ." James pointed out.

"It doesn't matter," Carina replied. "Better wet than kidnapped."

Without thinking twice, Carina, James, and Sarah bounded toward the creek and leaped in. The water was shallow and the current slow, so the friends weren't in much danger of getting swept away. But the uneven rocks at the bottom of the creek made navigating it tricky.

Carina held the satchel with Galileo's diary above her

head. She couldn't let it get wet or it would be ruined, and then she would never learn the secrets her father wanted her to study.

"There they are!" one of the men shouted from behind them. "The brats are crossing the water!"

James and Sarah reached the other bank before Carina did. She struggled to keep up, but drizzle had begun to fall, making it hard to see. And holding her satchel above her head was throwing her off-balance in the water.

"Hurry, Carina!" yelled James.

With a burst of effort, Carina pushed toward the other side. She never even saw the woman with the dark hair stepping up lightly behind her, balancing on the rocks like an acrobat.

"Ahhh!" Carina cried out in pain as something snagged her hair.

It was the woman. She yanked Carina back into the creek.

"James!" Carina screamed, and threw him her satchel just before tumbling back.

For a moment, everything was a blur of waves and bubbles and swirling water. Miraculously, Carina popped up above the surface, gasping for air. Only then did she realize the woman still held her by the hair.

Blinking and coughing, Carina looked frantically for her friends. She caught a glimpse of the men crossing to the other side and picking up James as if he weighed nothing. They grabbed Sarah, too. She fought back against her captors, and one hit her on the side of the head. Sarah went limp.

"No!" yelled Carina. Instantly, the woman pushed her below the water again. Carina panicked, her mouth filling before she'd even had a chance to catch a breath. She fought and wriggled and grasped desperately at the woman's hands holding her hair.

The woman pulled her up again, and Carina gasped as her head broke the surface.

"Be a good girl, now," the woman said calmly. "We need you alive."

* * *

The thugs dragged Carina, Sarah, and James to a makeshift camp set up in the woods. The drizzle had stopped by the time they reached it, and fire burned beside a tattered tent and wagon. The men roughly shoved all three of the children to the ground. The short one ripped Carina's satchel from James's grip while two of the others bound the children's hands behind them.

The monkey from the festival was there, waiting. Chattering, he circled around the children. To Carina, it sounded like laughter.

Sarah moaned. She'd been thrown closer to the fire than the others, with smoke billowing toward her. The girl's temple was bruised and swollen, and she was only half-conscious.

"What do you want with us?" Carina asked the rogues, more confidently than she felt.

None replied. The short one started rifling through Carina's satchel.

"Hey!" Carina yelled. "That's mine."

The man ignored her and withdrew Galileo's diary. He studied the ruby for a long moment before carefully plucking it from the cover and handing it to the monkey. Then he passed the book to the dark-haired woman.

"Tell me, child," the woman said. "How did you come across this?"

Carina didn't answer. She wasn't about to play along.

The short man stepped forward and slapped Carina's face. The force knocked her back. She gasped, stung, her cheek burning.

"You will speak when spoken to," he directed.

"Where did you get this?" the woman repeated.

"It is mine," Carina said though gritted teeth.

"You stole it?"

"My father gave it to me."

The woman knelt down in front of Carina, her face uncomfortably close. She pressed the spine of the book against Carina's cheek, pushing the girl's face awkwardly to one side. "There are legends about an old book with a ruby on the cover and a cluster of five stars," the woman spoke in a low voice. "The symbol of the *map*. Tell me, child, do you know what you have been carrying? Can you read the book?"

"Why do we waste time questioning them?" one of the rogues asked. He ripped the book from the dark-haired woman's grasp and flipped through the pages. "This book means nothing. It's scribbled in devil language. Let's take the ruby and go."

"Because the ruby is not the most valuable treasure here." The woman stared intently at Carina. "Isn't that right, child?"

Now Carina was extremely confused. *Legends? A map?* Still, she wasn't about to let on that she didn't know what they were referring to.

"You tell me," Carina said smartly. "Can *you* read it?"

The woman smiled. On her face, it was a dangerous expression.

"Our parents will come looking for us," James, next to Carina, piped up. "They'll be here soon."

At that, the men laughed.

"You think we are afraid of your parents, boy?" the short man said. "We did not travel across the sea and back, facing storms and soldiers, to be scared away by your mummy and daddy."

"You're pirates, then?" Carina guessed.

"We are wanderers," the woman said simply. "Who is your father, child?"

Without really thinking, Carina responded smoothly, "Galileo Galilei."

She watched the woman's expression. It didn't change. That meant she didn't know who Galileo Galilei was.

"And your father taught you of the map?" the woman asked.

"He taught me of many," Carina lied.

The woman frowned. "The legend speaks of only one."

"Are you sure?" Carina countered.

As she spoke, Carina's mind raced. She had absolutely no idea what the woman was talking about. But making it seem like she *did* was likely the only thing keeping them alive.

Think! Carina urged herself. *The men want the jewel, but the woman wants the book, because she thinks it's . . . legendary? Magic? The man said it's in devil language. They must all be superstitious. Very superstitious . . .*

Just then, something moved in the trees. It was large enough to make the branches shake. They all turned their heads at the noise.

"We are wasting time," one of the men said nervously. "There are strange creatures in these woods. Let's take the jewel and leave these brats here to their fate."

"He's right," said James. "There are wild animals in this forest. The kee—I mean, my parents told me so."

"I am sure you will see the animals soon enough," the

short man quipped. That made everyone laugh—even the monkey.

"I can read the book," Carina blurted out suddenly.

Everyone turned to look at her.

"The child can read the devil's language?" one of the men whispered to another.

"It's not the devil's language," said James. "It's—"

Carina elbowed him.

"Yes, I can," Carina said. "Let me read it, and you will see."

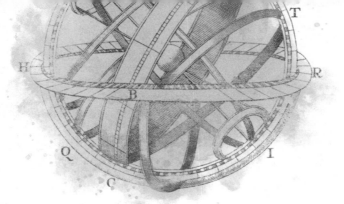

CHAPTER 8

THE MEN SHUFFLED NERVOUSLY. They didn't seem to like the idea of Carina's reading from the book.

But the woman looked intrigued. She studied Carina for a long moment. Then she knelt down and opened the diary in front of Carina.

"Speak, child," she said. "We are listening."

"This is not good," one of the men whispered to the short man. "Your seer—she is bringing dark magic upon us."

The monkey hissed.

"You are all fools," the dark-haired woman said. "You worry about a ruby when I offer you the path to untold fortune—the Map No Man Can Read."

"Dark magic!" the man whispered again, more urgently.

Picking up on all this, Carina pretended to read from the book. But she did so like she was incanting something sinister.

"Quando gli uccelli voleran fin sopra le stelle e le nuvole saran basse nel cielo, allora vedrete arcobaleni."

Only Carina knew what she had really said in her beginner's Italian: "When birds fly over the stars, and the clouds are low in the sky, then you will see rainbows."

The rustling in the branches grew more violent. Carina felt Sarah move beside her.

"I do not like this," the nervous man said. He snatched the ruby from the monkey, and the tiny creature snapped its teeth angrily. "We have what we came for," insisted the man. "Let's let this witch have her servant and get out of here."

Carina continued to chant louder and louder. She even began swaying for effect.

"La tempesta sta arrivando, e non potete fare nulla per fermarla. Vi bagnerete tutti!"

This time she said, "The storm is coming, and there is nothing you can do to stop it. You will get wet!"

That was when she saw a spark from a fiery stick Sarah was holding in her hands, which were now unbound. Sarah flung the stick at the man holding the ruby. His pants began to smolder.

"Do you smell something?" one of the rogues asked.

"Probably the monkey," another replied. "That thing is covered in flies."

Angry, the monkey jumped on the head of the man who had insulted him.

That was when the man holding the ruby noticed his burning pants.

"Yeeeeeeooooooooooow!" he cried, trying to snuff out the flame. "That witch child has set me on fire!"

"A fuoco! State andando a fuoco! Presto sarete tutti in fiamme!" Carina chanted as though possessed. The men had no way of knowing she was saying, "You are on fire! You are on fire! You will soon all be on fire!" But they were thoroughly unnerved anyway. Even the dark-haired woman was starting to look unsettled.

Sarah flicked another well-aimed piece of lit kindling.

Then the short man's jacket caught fire.

"This is the devil's work! What have you brought upon us?" he demanded of the dark-haired woman. "What should we do?"

The branches shook and swayed behind them. Carina let out a piercing scream. Then, abruptly, she stopped, staring upward, mouth gaping, eyes unfocused.

"I think you should run," James said simply.

The men all looked at one another. And they ran. The man whose pants were on fire dropped the ruby so he could smack at his burning behind with every awkward step.

The dark-haired woman glared at Carina—before tossing Galileo's diary into the fire and tuning to run as well.

"No!" yelled Carina, breaking from her fake trance. She dove for the book, desperate to knock it away from the flames. Her hands were still bound behind her, so she used her feet, her skirt brushing the edge of the flames.

"Carina, stop!" yelled Sarah. "You'll set yourself on fire!" She pulled her friend away with one hand, then snatched the book from the fire with the other. To Carina's relief, only the back cover of the book was a bit charred.

Carina stared at Sarah's unbound hands. "How did you get free?"

Sarah smiled. "I noticed the ropes were pretty loose when I came to. They must not have thought I was much of a threat," she said.

"That was incredible!" James exclaimed as Sarah helped both of them undo the rope from their wrists. "Carina, where did you learn to say all that stuff?"

Carina shrugged. "I was making most of it up, really. When I can't remember something the master asks me to say in my lessons, I make up something that sounds good. He is always very cross when I do that. But it came in handy here. Those men were clearly superstitious, so I thought we could use their silly talk of dark magic against them."

"I'll say," replied James, laughing. "It saved our skins!"

"Thanks to you." Carina looked at Sarah meaningfully.

Sarah smiled more widely than she had in months.

"And the branches!" James suddenly exclaimed. "How did you make those shake?"

"Uhhhhhhh . . ." said Carina. "I didn't. . . ."

Slowly, the friends turned to the branches that had been moving violently moments before. They continued to rustle and sway.

"Carina . . ." James said nervously.

The branches shook. Something scratched the tree trunk. And then . . .

Out popped three squirrels! They chased one another around the clearing before scurrying back up a tree into the darkness.

The friends released their breath and looked at one another.

"Well, that was lucky," James finally said.

Carina and Sarah laughed as they helped each other to their feet.

"It was indeed," said Carina.

* * *

That night, safely back at the children's home, Carina crouched next to an open window in one of the common areas, cradling Galileo's diary in her lap. Just as she had predicted, the keepers hadn't even noticed they were missing.

There had been too much revelry at Miss Esther's wedding, and all the keepers had returned in various states of sobriety.

They never even realized we were gone, Carina thought smugly. Then she felt a tiny pang. James had been right: no one had noticed. Not even one.

Shaking away the thought, Carina gingerly studied the charred diary cover. It wasn't burned too badly, though she would need to be extra careful with it from then on.

Suddenly, the wind picked up, and a strong breeze blew through the window. The pages of the diary turned on their own, opening to a drawing Carina had seen many times before.

A cluster of five stars was centered among a sea of black and white inked dots. Beneath it was a depiction of the ocean, with large sea creatures swimming through the depths. And at the bottom of the ocean floor was an object. Carina had never been able to figure out what it was. But it looked kind of like a spear with three prongs.

Carina gazed at the five stars burning bright on the page, turned back to the book's cover, and then turned to the drawing again.

"That woman spoke of the five stars," she murmured. "She said they were the symbol of 'the map.'"

Carina looked up from the drawing and out the children's home window, toward the stars.

"Tutte le verità saranno comprese quando le stesse si saranno

derectus," she whispered. "All truths will be understood once the stars align. This must be what the woman was talking about! Maybe it's the Map No Man Can Read. The one that leads to a great treasure." She could almost feel the cogs turning in her brain. "This is why my father wanted me to have the diary! He wanted me to study the stars so I can seek the treasure. *That* is my birthright!"

Carina grinned widely.

No matter what, no matter how long it took, she *was* going to read the map.

She promised herself that.

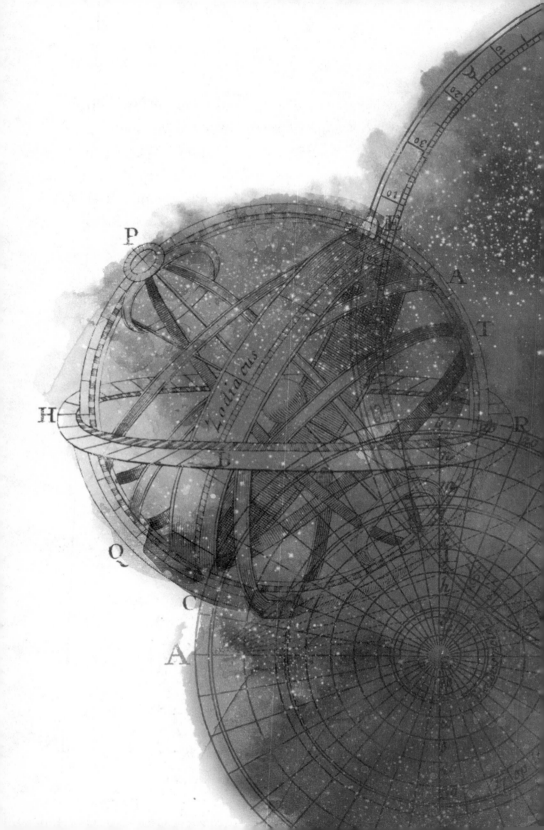

PART TWO

HANOVER HALL

Chapter 9

FIVE YEARS LATER, fourteen-year-old Carina Smyth studied herself in the mirror.

She didn't think she looked much different. Taller, yes, and perhaps her face was a bit thinner.

But her whole world was changing, and she didn't like it.

"Do I have to go?" she asked Mrs. Altwood.

The old woman helped Carina into a patched traveling cloak handed down by one of the local village girls. "You know as well as I do, child, there is nothing more for you here."

Carina noted the deep wrinkles that crossed Mrs. Altwood's face. The past five years had taken a toll on the woman, and she looked worse for the wear. Carina felt bad that some—most?—of the wrinkles might have been caused by her.

"But will there be anything for me there?" Carina asked pointedly. "I have been working so hard to read Galileo's diary and study the stars the way my father intended me to, all to be sent off as a servant in some dusty, forgotten hall."

Mrs. Altwood tsked. "Carina Smyth, will you ever learn to curb your tongue?" It was not really a question, but more of a beleaguered observation.

"I do not think so." Carina gave a wry half smile. "But I blame you. You should have whipped me when there was still a chance to knock some sense into me."

That made the old woman chuckle.

"Yes, I suppose I should have," Mrs. Altwood said. "You do realize, child, how fortunate an opportunity this is for you? Lord Willoughby has taken a particular interest in your future. He has placed you at a hall where he thinks you will be a good fit. You will be cared for—safe. Surely your father would have wanted that?"

Carina nodded. "I appreciate all that Lord Willoughby has done for me. Truly I do. Yet still . . ." She placed a hand on Galileo's diary, which lay on the bed. "The more I learn from this, the more I can't shake the feeling my father wanted something bigger for me. Something greater. Something . . . extraordinary."

"Your head is in the stars again, child," Mrs. Altwood

chided. "It is time to come back down to Earth. If your father was truly a man of science, he would have been practical. He would have wanted safety and security for you. This placement offers you that."

Carina looked at herself in the mirror again. Her hair was pulled back into a braided twist like Sarah's had been a few years prior. The girls had managed to rebuild their friendship, at least enough that they were sad to part when Sarah was sent to work as a servant in the couple of years following their adventure in the woods. James, meanwhile, had been apprenticed out to a carpenter in the village, largely thanks to Carina's efforts. She had noticed a sign announcing that the master carpenter was searching for an apprentice, and Carina had encouraged James to make his case to the keepers. That had been one year earlier. Carina and James had kept in touch in the beginning, but the master carpenter had moved to London and taken James with him. Since then, Carina had not heard from her friends—either of them.

"Do you know anything more of where I am being sent?" Carina asked. "Anything at all?"

"I'm afraid not," Mrs. Altwood said. "Lady Devonshire of Hanover Hall requires a housemaid. Lord Willoughby has met Her Ladyship and seemed to think that the placement would be keenly suited to you. I believe I have read the name Devonshire before, in the society pages. She must be a woman of great stature. I am certain you will get on there."

She leaned forward, smiling warmly at Carina. "And you will make friends."

Carina frowned. "I am not so certain." She hoisted the satchel with Galileo's diary over her head and across her shoulder. "Something tells me an estate called Hanover Hall does not take kindly to servants with uncurbed tongues."

"I daresay not." Mrs. Altwood nodded. "Yet I doubt that will deter you?"

Carina smiled. "I daresay not."

She took the old woman's hands.

"Will you pass along any letters to me that arrive here?" Carina asked.

"Of course," Mrs. Altwood promised. "Have you had any word from Sarah or James?"

"No," Carina admitted. "I would have thought they would write. At least to me."

"Not many of the children write once they leave," Mrs. Altwood said. "It's the way things are. They move on."

"I will write to you," Carina promised.

"I would like that very much," Mrs. Altwood replied.

* * *

The carriage rumbled along the bumpy road. Carina sat in the back, a worn travel bag resting in her lap and her satchel tucked safely at her side. The driver sent by Lady

Devonshire's estate had been surprised when he saw the girl had no more luggage than a carpetbag.

"Are you not joining Hanover Hall's employ indefinitely?" the driver had asked, raising an eyebrow.

"I am," Carina had replied simply. Then she had mumbled under her breath, "I suppose Lady Devonshire is not in the habit of hiring orphans."

Carina had watched the gray landscape tumble by for several hours. Barren moors dotted with sparse trees and rocks came and went. On the horizon, a collection of dark clouds indicated an approaching storm.

"Driver, how long until we reach the hall?" Carina called up from the window.

"Not long now, miss," he replied. "We are almost there."

Carina looked out again at the bleak landscape. Perched on a solitary tree several yards away, a large crow cawed.

That did not bode well.

Finally, some overgrown landscaping and shrubs broke the empty road. The carriage turned a bend, and ahead loomed a stately stone manor.

"Welcome to Hanover Hall," the driver said.

Carina leaned out the window and caught her breath. The estate was massive—far larger than any building she had seen in her life. It was three stories high, with tall windows that lined the outside marking each level. Towers resembling castle turrets anchored the building's four corners. And a large circular fountain on the front grounds reflected the sinking sun.

"It's enormous," Carina breathed. Then she panicked. "Am I to service the *entire* estate?"

"Of course," the driver replied lightly. Seeing the stricken look that crossed Carina's face, he backtracked. "Only joking, miss. You will be one of many servants at Hanover."

Carina sighed and looked back at the hall. One of the corner towers had a window open at the very top. Something in the window glinted—a silver tube? Carina craned her neck to get a better look.

"We're here." The driver pulled to an abrupt halt in front of the hall and hopped down. "If you'll follow me, miss . . ."

Carina trudged after the man to the looming wooden doors of the estate. He pounded the large knocker, and a middle-aged servant answered.

"I've brought the new hire," the driver announced. "Miss . . ."

"Carina Smyth," Carina said.

"Yes, of course." The servant looked dull and sullen. "Right this way."

Carina followed the woman inside and gave a last fleeting look out the doors before the driver shut them securely.

"I am Mrs. Rossi," the servant said.

"Carina Smyth," Carina said, introducing herself again brightly. "Pleased to meet you."

Mrs. Rossi seemed neither pleased nor concerned with further pleasantries. "Follow me," she said, turning away.

Carina raised an eyebrow. "A pleasure, I'm sure," she mumbled.

Mrs. Rossi immediately began a tour of the estate. Carina hurried to keep up while still balancing her bag and satchel as the woman bustled from room to room.

"This is the sitting room." Mrs. Rossi gestured to an elegant parlor with several ornate chairs. Each one was framed in wood with a symbol of the sun and moon carved at the top. "Lady Devonshire receives her guests in here. You will be responsible for morning tea and keeping the fires going. You are not to enter the room when Her Ladyship is there. Ever. Is that understood?"

"Yes," Carina said, a little bewildered. "May I ask why?"

Mrs. Rossi stopped abruptly and looked Carina up and down, as if seeing her for the first time. She eyed Carina's worn carpetbag and cloak.

"Where did you say you have come to us from again?" she asked.

"The most esteemed estate known as Benevolent Children's Home Hall," Carina quipped.

Mrs. Rossi did not laugh.

Carina cleared her throat. "I mean to say that I was previously in Lord Willoughby's service," she fibbed.

Mrs. Rossi looked her up and down again. "We will

provide you with proper attire. And I will warn you, Hanover Hall does not take kindly to humor."

Mrs. Rossi's shoes *click-clack*ed as she walked on. Carina cracked her neck uncomfortably. "No, I daresay it does not."

Mrs. Rossi led Carina to the drawing room, the dining room, the great hall, and, finally, the kitchen and servants' quarters.

"You will sleep here, along with Miss Celia." Mrs. Rossi brought Carina to a cramped chamber with two cots. She pointed to a girl a few years older than Carina seated at the edge of the room. Celia was adjusting her hair cap and offered Carina a halfhearted wave. She, too, looked rather downtrodden.

Mrs. Rossi opened a drawer and began tossing fresh clothing onto Carina's sleeping cot.

"When will I meet Lady Devonshire?" Carina asked.

Mrs. Rossi stopped mid-toss, her mouth agape. "My goodness, things must have been different where you came from," she said. "Her Ladyship does not converse with the staff. It is highly unlikely you will meet her at all, unless something is amiss."

"Not meet her at all?" Now Carina's mouth dropped. "You mean I am never to meet my employer? What if something is wrong that needs addressing?"

"If something is wrong," Mrs. Rossi said tightly, "you will address it with me."

Carina opened her mouth to respond and then promptly shut it.

"It wasn't always like this," Celia commented. "It used to be better when Master—"

"Celia!" Mrs. Rossi snapped suddenly. "That is enough. Go see that the fires have been tended, *par favore.*"

"Yes, Mrs. Rossi," Celia replied, hurrying away.

Carina had perked up at Mrs. Rossi's pointed last phrase. "Are you Italian?"

"I am," Mrs. Rossi replied.

"Have you ever heard of Galileo Galilei?" Carina asked eagerly. "He was an Italian man of science."

"What in heaven's name compels you to speak of 'men of science'?" Mrs. Rossi asked coldly. "Carina—Smyth, you said?—I believe we must get one thing quite clear. You are now in the employ of Hanover Hall. All concerns from wherever you came from are no longer pertinent. You will tend the fires, clean the hall, and serve tea. From now on, I suggest you keep all questions to yourself and only speak when spoken to. Is that understood?"

Carina swallowed hard. If she hadn't liked the idea of her life changing before, she loathed it now.

"Yes, it is," she said.

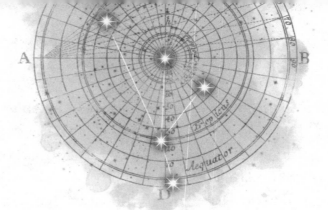

Chapter 10

THE HOURS WERE LONG and the days even longer at Hanover Hall. Carina mastered her duties easily, mainly because there wasn't much thinking involved. The routine was always the same: open windows, light fires, prep tea, serve tea (but never in Lady Devonshire's presence), clean away tea, tidy sitting room, straighten great hall, sweep floors, wash floors, dust, dust, dust, empty chamber pots, prep tea, serve tea, clean away tea, repeat.

Carina didn't mind the manual labor. After fourteen years at children's homes, hard work was nothing new to her. Plus, there were thirty or so servants at the hall and everyone worked just as diligently as she did. She wrote to Mrs.

Altwood when she could, but it was becoming challenging to think of new things to say about her life at Hanover Hall.

It was all just so *boring*.

Not once did Carina even catch a glimpse of Lady Devonshire. Well, that wasn't exactly true. Once—*once*—she could have sworn she saw the train of the lady's gown sweep around a corner. But other than that, nothing. As far as Carina knew, none of the servants aside from Mrs. Rossi and maybe a select other few had met the woman. The tea was always to be left at a specific time and the sitting room promptly exited. An hour later, the tea would have mysteriously vanished, and the cups remained to be cleared away. Her Ladyship took all her meals in her chambers. All mail was to be left outside Her Ladyship's door. If any visitors came, notice was delivered by handwritten note. More often than not, they were sent away either empty-handed or with a brief note from Her Ladyship (also slid under the door).

Carina wasn't even sure what Lady Devonshire *looked* like. There were no portraits hanging in Hanover Hall. On her second day working there, Carina noticed a rectangular bit of wallpaper over the mantel in the sitting room that looked brighter than the rest.

"What used to hang there?" she'd asked one of the other housemaids.

The fellow servant hadn't replied.

Everyone seemed on edge to Carina. Lunch and dinner were quiet affairs. The servants ate their food in silence. Occasionally one of the house stewards would rustle a newspaper. No one received mail. No one came and went. It was as though a dark cloud had settled on the estate, sucking up any merriment that might have been.

"Does anyone here ever . . . laugh?" Carina asked Celia one day.

"Laugh?" Celia replied, as if the word were strange to her.

Carina blinked. "You know—ha, ha, ha?"

"I know what it means to laugh," Celia responded. "But no, now that you mention it, I suppose not." She tilted her head to one side. "It used to be different. I liked it better then."

"What *happened* here?" Carina asked bluntly.

Celia stared off, transfixed by a memory. "Her Ladyship was happy then. We used to wait for the mail eagerly—news from the university. There were always carriers coming and going. And fires burning late into the night that needed tending."

"So you've seen her?" Carina asked, delighted finally to be gaining some information. "You've seen Lady Devonshire?"

"Oh, yes," Celia said. "I'm probably one of the only ones who has. Well, me and Mrs. Rossi. Everyone else had to be replaced. Her Ladyship was never the same . . . after."

"What happened?" Carina repeated urgently. "What terrible tragedy occurred to make everyone so sullen?"

Celia suddenly snapped out of her chatty mood. She looked around. "Mrs. Rossi will have my neck if I say any more," she said nervously. "She and I are the only two originals left, and it's because we've learned to hold our tongues." Celia looked Carina up and down. "You should learn to hold yours if you want to stay. Or you'll end up like all the others—handed a note informing you of your dismissal, and your bag thrown out on the front step."

* * *

Three months passed. Autumn changed to winter, and the days grew abysmally short. But the one good thing about longer nights was that Carina had more time to look out the window, studying the stars. Late into the evening, after the other servants had gone to bed, Carina would sneak away and draw close to the sitting room window. It was tall with clear glass, and on a good night, she could gaze out the window for hours, memorizing the stars that were out with Galileo's diary in her lap.

Sometimes she could even match up the constellations from the diary diagrams with what she saw in the sky. There were Ursa Major and Ursa Minor. And Andromeda and Perseus. One of Carina's favorites was Orion. Galileo often referred to it in his diary.

She still hadn't figured out how to see the map, exactly. But after studying with the master for five years and learning to read Italian fluently, Carina had a pretty good idea where to look—the stars! Galileo had believed the Map No Man Can Read was hidden in the stars. He had made references to a powerful ancient treasure—the Trident of Poseidon. Carina assumed that must be the spear-like object at the bottom of the ocean in the picture. Now she was positive she knew why her father had left her the diary: it was her birthright to seek out the map and follow it to the Trident of Poseidon. The question was, *how* was she supposed to find a map hidden in the stars?

One particularly cold night, Carina sat nestled up against the window with a shawl around her shoulders and the diary in her lap. The fire in the sitting room had long since burned out, but she couldn't relight it without risking attention. She stayed there in the dark, looking up at the stars, reading the book by the light of the moon.

Suddenly, she heard a noise in the hall.

Carina stayed perfectly still, barely breathing.

A moment passed, and Carina crept to the doorway to peek around the corner.

Carina caught a glimpse of a woman with gray hair up the stairs on the second floor, moving away from the hall that led to Lady Devonshire's chambers. Holding a glowing candelabra, the woman passed along silently, turning a corner toward a staircase to the third level. The glow slowly faded, sending everything back into darkness.

Carina had never seen this woman at the estate before. That could mean only one thing.

"Lady Devonshire," she whispered to herself.

Carina knew there was only one choice. She should sneak back to the servants' quarters while she still could, and avoid being spotted. She should go to sleep and forget she had seen anything. It would be safer that way.

Carina smiled.

Yes, there was only one choice, really.

Carina tiptoed to the staircase and followed the woman with the glowing candelabra.

CHAPTER 11

CARINA TRAILED THE WOMAN up one flight of stairs and then another. They climbed up and up, to a part of the estate Carina had never been in before. All the while, Lady Devonshire's candelabra glowed softly, illuminating the shadowed wall.

Carina barely breathed. She wasn't exactly sure what she was doing. But there was a shroud of secrecy over Hanover Hall, and something about that lit a fire inside her. She felt compelled to follow the woman and solve the mystery.

They reached the top of the third staircase. Carina kept a safe distance, noting doorways and protrusions from the walls that she could hide behind in case Lady Devonshire turned around. But the woman seemed completely absorbed.

She didn't even look from side to side as she walked—just straight ahead.

Lady Devonshire turned a corner, and Carina waited an extra moment or two before peeking around. When she did, she frowned. The hall was long—very long—with tall windows and no doors. There wouldn't be anywhere to hide if Lady Devonshire looked back.

Carina took a deep breath. She pressed forward.

The full moon shone through the long glass panes, casting the opposing wall in a soft blue glow. Something caught Carina's eye. She gasped.

There was a person standing in a recess in the wall!

With a fright, Carina jumped back, stifling a cry. A moment later, she let out her breath.

It wasn't a person—just a life-sized statue on display.

"For goodness' sake," she mumbled to herself.

She carefully stepped forward. The statue was of a man with shoulder-length hair dressed in long robes. In one hand he held a strange-looking object: a series of spheres tilted around a central orb.

I've seen that before, Carina realized. Galileo had drawn a picture of one in his diary and had labeled it *armilla.*

Maybe this statue is of a man who studied the stars . . . like Galileo! Carina thought excitedly.

There was a plaque with a name at the base of the statue. Carina read it.

"'Nicolaus Copernicus.'"

Hmmmm, Carina thought. She didn't recognize the name, but it sounded important.

She crept forward down the hall. Another statue stood in a recess.

" 'Sir Isaac Newton,' " she read softly from the plaque. That name she *had* heard before. The Italian master had mentioned it to her once or twice when she'd referenced something scientific from Galileo's diary. "You are not Sir Isaac Newton's daughter," he'd admonish her, "so stop playing like you are."

Carina's eyes grew wide. "These statues are *all* men of science."

A third statue stood just ahead. Lady Devonshire had almost reached the end of the hall. But Carina was fascinated and wanted to see more. She stepped forward to take a closer look.

A lump formed in her throat.

"It can't be," she whispered.

Standing in front of her, real enough that she could reach out and take his hand, was a life-sized statue of the man she had spent her whole life studying.

GALILEO GALILEI, the plaque read.

"Is this truly him?" she asked, placing a palm on the statue. This sculpture also wore long robes, but it had a chiseled beard and short hair. It stood in a pose as though pondering the heavens, a rolled-up parchment in one hand. And at its feet was . . . a sculpture of the diary. *Her* diary. Galileo Galilei's diary!

Carina looked from the sculpture to the diary in her hands and then back to the sculpture. It was as though things were falling into place. Galileo Galilei wasn't just a shadowy image anymore. She was seeing him for the first time. A true man of science. A student of the stars. The man her father wanted her to learn from.

"What is this place?" she asked herself, overcome.

Carina looked down the hall at Lady Devonshire. The woman was ascending a winding flight of stairs at the end.

Carina swiftly tiptoed after her. At the staircase, she stopped. There was no way to follow now without being seen. She'd have to wait at the bottom.

Carina watched as Lady Devonshire reached a large wooden door at the top of the spiral staircase. The woman placed her hand on the doorknob and paused. She stayed there for a long moment before sinking her chin toward her breast and resting her forehead against the door.

Carina furrowed her brow. What was the woman doing?

Then, as though changing her mind about the entire excursion, Lady Devonshire turned and began to descend the stairs.

Oh, no! thought Carina. *Oh, no, oh, no, oh, no!*

She hurried away before Lady Devonshire could spot her. But the hallway was too long. She'd never reach the end in time. She was going to get caught!

I have to hide! Carina thought urgently. *But where? There isn't anywhere!*

She looked desperately back and forth across the long hall. The tall windows seemed to mock her with the amount of moonlight they threw across the passageway. And there was barely any space beside the statues in the wall recesses. Even a child would have a hard time squeezing in. . . .

Except for in a spot next to the statue of Galileo, Carina realized. The way his robes were carved left a wider opening to one side than the others had. But could she fit?

Without taking time to think about it, Carina made herself as tiny as possible and squeezed into the space beside Galileo Galilei's statue. She pulled her skirts in alongside her just as the light from the woman's candelabra spilled into the hallway.

Carina waited, her heart pounding. She couldn't hear Lady Devonshire coming. She couldn't even see her. But the light from the candelabra grew stronger.

Carina held her breath and closed her eyes. The candlelight flashed, and rustling skirts whooshed by. Then nothing. The sounds receded and disappeared.

A few moments later, Carina ventured a look around the corner. The hall was empty.

"Heavens." Carina let out her breath. "That was close."

She turned back to face the doorway leading to the spiral staircase.

She should really, *really* go back to the servants' quarters now.

She did not.

Instead, Carina walked back and ascended the stairs to the heavy wooden door. She tried the knob. It was locked.

Frowning, Carina bent down to peer through the large keyhole. She didn't think she'd be able to see much through the tiny opening, but she was mistaken.

Moonlight flooded the room beyond. From her vantage point, Carina could make out a curved wall completely composed of windows facing the door. She couldn't see much of the floor, but it looked like there were many objects scattered about.

And then . . .

"I don't believe it."

Propped up against the windows was a telescope. A *huge* telescope. Carina had only seen drawings of them in Galileo's diary. And they had been tiny—more like spyglasses. But with an instrument such as this, Carina could not only observe the heavens; she could *study* them.

I need to get in there! she thought wildly.

Throwing caution to the wind, Carina plucked a hairpin from her hair and tinkered with the keyhole. She'd picked more than her fair share of locks at the children's home. Surely this one wouldn't be any—

Click!

"Success!" whispered Carina. Her heart raced as she turned the doorknob and stepped into the room.

What she saw took her breath away.

The room was no mere study. It was a complete observatory!

"Incredible!" she exclaimed. "Those are compasses . . . and that is a quadrant. Is that—it can't be—it is! A mechanized planetarium!"

Carina marveled as she spun, gazing at all the instruments she'd only read about in Galileo's diary. Telescopes and armillary spheres and astrolabes. Tools Carina never thought she would see in person, let alone have access to.

"This . . . this . . ." Tears welled despite her. "This is . . . everything."

She never even heard the footsteps ascending the staircase behind her.

CHAPTER 12

"HOW DARE YOU!" A woman's shrill voice pierced through the doorway.

Carina whirled around.

Lady Devonshire stood, seething, in the entrance. Her eyes flared with anger fiercer than the candelabra's fire.

"L-Lady Devonshire," Carina stammered. "I can explain—"

"How *dare* you!" the woman shrieked. "Get out of here, now! Get out, get out, *get out!*"

Carina didn't try to argue. She raced past the woman and flew down the staircase. She ran back through the hall, down every flight of stairs, and all the way back to the servants' quarters. She stopped running only when she'd reached the door to her room. Leaning heavily against the wall, she caught her breath.

I'm done for, she thought miserably. She half expected that at any moment she would hear, thundering behind her, the footsteps of men or guards prepared to take her away in the night.

She had messed up. Badly. There was no way she would be allowed to stay.

And yet that room—*that room.* It held within it everything Carina had ever wanted. Everything she could ever have hoped for, all in one place.

What am I going to do? she thought. *I can't leave. Not when I'm so close.*

A sound in the hall caught her attention. A cold sweat broke over her. As swiftly as she could, Carina whisked her door open and slipped inside.

Celia was in bed, sound asleep. Carina listened against the door for any more noises in the hall, but all she could hear was Celia's soft snoring.

Quietly, Carina changed into her nightclothes and climbed into bed.

"I must speak with Lady Devonshire in the morning," she whispered to herself, determined. "I will show her the diary. Somehow I will convince her to let me stay and let me see that room again."

But with every sound that night, Carina's heart pounded.

She did not sleep, convinced they would come to take her away before daylight.

* * *

Morning finally came. Carina glanced at herself in the mirror. She looked terrible. Dark circles pooled under her eyes, and she couldn't stop yawning.

"Are you ill?" Celia asked. "You look positively dreadful."

"I am fine." Carina yawned again. "I did not sleep well."

Celia left the room as usual, but Carina cautiously poked her head around the doorframe before exiting. The housemaids and stewards bustled around with their morning duties.

Carina was on edge as she walked to the servants' dining hall for breakfast. But everything seemed normal. No one spoke. No one laughed. Just as plain and dull as ever. If every event from the prior evening hadn't been imprinted on Carina's memory, she would have thought it all a dream.

Carina reached her place at the table, and she stopped. Her heart sank.

A small square of folded paper rested on her plate. Carina picked it up and read the single line: YOU ARE HEREBY DISMISSED. YOU WILL LEAVE IMMEDIATELY.

Celia looked over Carina's shoulder and gasped.

"What in heaven's name did you do?" she asked.

Carina shook her head, fighting back tears. "I do not know," she lied.

Mrs. Rossi cleared her throat and walked over. She leaned down and spoke in a low, matter-of-fact tone. "There was only one servant who matched Lady Devonshire's description of the maid trespassing on her private quarters, and that is you. You will come with me and pack your bag. The driver will be waiting."

* * *

"I must speak with Lady Devonshire," Carina pleaded as Mrs. Rossi flung Carina's meager belongings into the carpetbag. "There must have been a misunderstanding."

"Out of the question," Mrs. Rossi replied curtly. "Once a servant has been dismissed, there is no further discussion."

"But that's not fair," Carina insisted. "If I may just speak with her, she will see—"

"She will see nothing." Mrs. Rossi snapped Carina's bag shut. "Do you think you are the first housemaid to be dismissed? I have seen men and women come and go—servants far worthier than you—who to this day do not know the reason for their dismissal. Her Ladyship's decisions are final. You will leave this morning, or we shall have the authorities summoned to drag you off the premises."

Carina stopped arguing. Pushing back against Mrs. Rossi would get her nowhere.

She'd have to take matters into her own hands.

Without another word, Carina picked up her bag and the satchel with Galileo's diary and walked with Mrs. Rossi out of the room.

A slew of servants had gathered to watch. They whispered, but none attempted to ask Carina what was happening.

Carina clutched her bags tighter and continued walking, past the dining room, past the great hall, and, finally, past the sitting room.

That was when she noticed another housemaid heading away. Morning tea must have been served for Her Ladyship—which meant Lady Devonshire was entering the sitting room right then, through the private entrance from her chambers.

Without a word, Carina darted to the right and ran straight to the sitting room doors.

"What in heaven's name—?" Mrs. Rossi cried. "Stop! Immediately!"

But Carina did not stop. She raced up and flung the doors open.

The woman from the night before—Lady Devonshire—sat inside. In the light of day, Carina could make out more of her appearance. The woman was dressed in a simple but elegant navy morning gown with a shawl about her shoulders. She was not old; her skin was smooth and her eyes keenly alert. Carina would have guessed she was not more than forty were it not for the shock of stately gray hair piled atop her head.

Lady Devonshire started, nearly spilling her tea. "How—"

"Dare I, yes, I know," Carina said. She needed to get straight to the point. "Your Ladyship, I have in my possession Galileo's diary." Carina quickly displayed the book, allowing the ruby to catch the morning light. "It was given to me by my father. I was abandoned as an infant with no other birthright than this—to study the stars. I swear, I did not know about the observatory nor realize what was in the room until last night. But now that I do—Your Ladyship, it was no accident I was placed here. Lord Willoughby was my benefactor. He must have sent me here on purpose—to study with you. To learn the heavens as my father intended me to."

Carina caught her breath, expecting Lady Devonshire to interrupt. But the woman did not. She maintained a frigid look, eyes locked with Carina's.

"Please, Your Ladyship," Carina begged, holding out the diary. "This must mean something. We can find out, together."

The other servants had all gathered outside the doors. Suddenly, two stewards stormed into the room. They grabbed Carina by her shoulders, hauling her back.

"Your Ladyship, do not send me away!" Carina shouted. "We can help one another!"

Lady Devonshire remained icily silent as the stewards dragged Carina out of the sitting room. They shoved her through the front entrance and threw her unceremoniously to the ground. Carina tumbled, hitting her head against the frozen dirt as the diary flew from her grasp.

Mrs. Rossi stepped up to the door. She tossed Carina's bag alongside her.

"Go," was all she said.

Carina watched as the heavy doors slammed. She wiped grit from her mouth. Her hands stung bitterly.

"I . . ." She shivered.

She looked hopefully to the window of the sitting room. But no one was there.

"Fine," Carina said to herself. She struggled to her feet unsteadily and picked up the diary.

For a moment, she glanced up at the tower with the observatory. *To be so close,* she thought.

Swallowing hard, she dusted herself off and wrapped her patched cloak more tightly around herself. There was no driver as promised. She was on her own.

So she began walking.

Past the leafless trees. Past the untended shrubs. And she was moving through the front gates leading to the moors when . . .

"Miss Carina! Miss Carina!"

Carina turned to see Celia running up to her on the path.

"You won't believe it," Celia panted, out of breath. "Lady Devonshire. She wishes to speak with you."

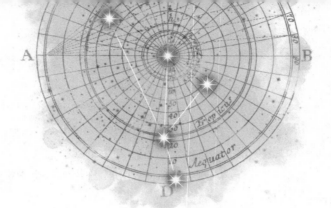

CHAPTER 13

IF THERE HAD BEEN MANY SERVANTS GATHERED in the hall before, now the entire staff had turned out to see what was happening. Every housemaid, chambermaid, cook, and steward watched intently as Carina was led back to Her Ladyship's sitting room. Carina guessed that it was likely the most excitement Hanover Hall had seen in, well, forever. She noted Mrs. Rossi standing at the front of the crowd, her face stony.

Carina stepped into the sitting room. Lady Devonshire was still seated exactly where she'd been before.

"Leave us," Her Ladyship instructed the stewards.

They bowed and turned away. The younger of the two

glanced back at Lady Devonshire. It was clearly his first time ever seeing his employer, and he appeared fascinated.

The moment the door shut, Carina spoke. "Your Ladyship, I—"

Lady Devonshire held up a hand to silence Carina. "The book," she said.

When Carina didn't respond, the woman raised her eyebrows expectantly. "Bring it here."

Carina hesitated. Then she withdrew Galileo's diary and handed it to Lady Devonshire.

The woman began carefully turning the pages.

"You say your father gave you this book?"

"Yes, my lady," Carina replied.

"And you do not know who your father is?"

"No, my lady," Carina said.

"Yet you can read it?"

Carina couldn't help huffing a little. "Of course, my lady."

Lady Devonshire looked up sharply. "It would behoove you to curb your tongue. Do you realize how much trouble you find yourself in?"

Carina opened her mouth to respond and then closed it again. She had a feeling that speaking further would only make things worse.

A hint of the vicious anger from the previous evening crossed Lady Devonshire's face. "Perhaps you feel that your intrusion last night was merely a trifle. I assure you, it was not." She held Carina's gaze for a painfully long moment. Finally, she looked down to turn the pages of the book. "Tell me, what do you hope to accomplish with this?"

"I—" Carina swallowed. "I wish to study the stars."

"That is a fool's effort," Lady Devonshire replied with some force. "You are a woman. You will never be allowed to study science, much less the stars."

"But you did," Carina said hopefully.

Lady Devonshire stopped turning the pages. "What makes you think that?"

"The observatory," Carina replied.

"You assume it is mine?"

"Isn't it?"

Lady Devonshire didn't answer. She had reached the drawing of the Trident of Poseidon and the Map No Man Can Read.

"I will require this book for perusal," she said abruptly.

Carina's heart pounded. "But—you can't—"

Lady Devonshire's eyes flashed. "I can't what? Speak up."

Carina's cheeks burned. But she forced herself to speak calmly. "My lady, I cannot part with the book. It is my birthright. I have fought my whole life to keep it."

"Do you really think you could stop me from keeping it as recompense for your transgression if I wished?" Lady Devonshire asked.

Carina wanted to reply heatedly. But something about Lady Devonshire's phrasing gave her pause. The woman was not like the Mr. Conways or Mrs. Rossis of the world. Her intentions ran deeper. She was testing her.

Carina chose her next words carefully. "If you wished?" she finally asked.

Her Ladyship stared at Carina for a long moment.

"You are fortunate that I do not intend to take your book," she finally spoke. "Merely to study it, in your own words."

"But how?" Carina asked. "If I am to be sent away?"

"Against my better instincts, I will permit you to keep your position at Hanover Hall," Lady Devonshire said. "In return, I will maintain access to this book indefinitely."

For one of the rare times in her life, Carina was uncertain what to say. "I . . . But . . . It's in Italian," she stammered.

If Carina hadn't known any better, she would have sworn Lady Devonshire's eyes twinkled with amusement.

"So you find it easy to believe I have studied the stars, but incomprehensible that I can read Italian?"

Again, Carina was rendered speechless.

Lady Devonshire closed the diary firmly. "I believe we have an understanding. You will return to your duties at once. But mark my words—if I ever hear of or see you putting one toe over the line again, you will be gone. Is that understood?"

Carina nodded. "Yes, my lady."

"Good," said Lady Devonshire. "My lady's maid will send written instructions regarding this book, which I will begin perusing immediately."

Somehow, the stewards knew it was time to open the doors. Carina watched as they walked in. But this time, they did not apprehend her.

Lady Devonshire nodded. "That is all."

* * *

"You do not know how lucky you are!" Celia whispered to Carina in their room. "No one has ever come back once dismissed—*ever*!"

"I'm not entirely certain what happened," Carina admitted. She hated being separated from Galileo's diary, even if it was temporary. It felt like a piece of her was missing. Still, she had no reason to doubt Lady Devonshire's intentions. And if it meant there was even the slightest chance she might get back into that observatory . . .

"What did you think of her?" Celia asked eagerly.

Carina thought. "She was not unpleasant. But brusque. And"—Carina remembered the wild look in the woman's eyes the night before—"troubled."

Celia nodded, as though she understood.

"But you know more about her than I," said Carina. "Tell me what happened here. What made Lady Devonshire this way?"

Celia and Carina looked up as Mrs. Rossi entered the room.

"I daresay I cannot be as loose with my tongue as you," Celia whispered once Mrs. Rossi was out of earshot. "I do not think I would be granted a second chance."

The girls watched Mrs. Rossi drop a basket of linens to be ironed on a cot on the other side of the room.

"I hope we can get on," Carina said, standing, her tone a bit more antagonistic than it probably should have been.

Mrs. Rossi looked at her. "Do you think I care whether you are here or not?"

Carina was unsure how to respond.

"My responsibility is to my job, as should be yours," Mrs. Rossi continued. "I have little concern for your fate as long as it does not affect mine."

The woman walked briskly out of the room and clicked the door shut.

"She's not all that bad," Celia said, helping Carina pick up the linens. "She used to have friends, but now she just keeps to herself, really."

"Yes, I've seen," Carina said, thinking back on the prior three months of dull repetitiveness. "It seems everyone here could use a change."

"What are you going to do?" Celia asked keenly. "We heard you say you wished to study the stars. Do you think you ever will?"

Carina's old mischievous half smile returned.

"I have a plan," she said.

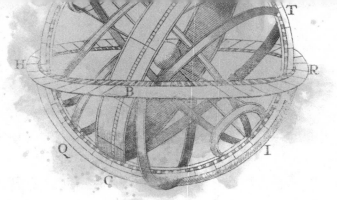

CHAPTER 14

THE INSTRUCTIONS from Lady Devonshire's lady's maid were brief and precise.

Carina was to drop off Galileo's diary every morning with Her Ladyship's tea. The book would be returned to Carina that evening via her lady's maid. If Her Ladyship desired to retain the book overnight, notice would be given that evening via handwritten message.

All else was to go back to the way it had been. Carina would not see Her Ladyship. She would not converse with her. The only change was the daily passing off of the book.

But that was all Carina needed.

She started with a simple note at first. A torn piece of paper slipped inside the front cover.

Andromeda was particularly bright last night, was it not?

She eagerly awaited the book's return that evening. The moment it was in her hands, she looked through every page to see if there was a return note.

To her dismay, there was not.

Yet . . . her slip of paper was gone.

Her notes on the days following were similar.

Orion will be coming into view this evening.

What did you think of Galileo's passage on the phases of Venus?

Heliocentrism makes perfect sense, to my mind.

Each day the diary was returned to her without a reply note, yet her original piece of paper was gone. And Carina couldn't help noticing that when her note referred to an upcoming celestial event, those were the evenings Lady Devonshire sent word she would be retaining the book until the next day.

A month passed, and Carina felt it was time. The note she slipped in the book that morning was different.

Have you reached the Map No Man Can Read?

She waited more anxiously than ever for the diary's return that evening. When the knock came at her door, she practically leaped from the bed.

Her heart raced as she opened the cover. A small square of paper fell to the floor.

Yes, it read.

A huge grin broke across Carina's face. Her plan was working! Now for her ultimate message.

The next morning, Carina's hand shook as she wrote her favorite line from the diary: *Tutte le verità saranno comprese quando le stesse si saranno derectus.*

All that day, Carina could barely concentrate on her usual duties, eagerly awaiting the return of the book.

It felt like an eternity before the knock finally came that evening.

But when Carina opened the door, it was not the lady's maid with the book as usual. It was a steward.

"Her Ladyship requests your presence in the sitting room," he said. "Follow me."

Chapter 15

CARINA COULDN'T HELP BOUNCING a little in place while the steward announced her. The possibility of what it could mean—of all her hopes culminating in one fateful meeting—was elating and terrifying and overwhelming all at once.

Carina gave a small curtsy as she entered the room. Her Ladyship was dressed in a stately violet dressing gown with lace at the cuffs. Her gray hair was pulled up in a twist.

"I imagine you are curious why I summoned you?" Lady Devonshire said once the steward left the room.

"I imagine it is because of my note," Carina replied, barely containing her excitement.

Lady Devonshire held Galileo's diary in her lap, open to

the page with the Map No Man Can Read. *"'Tutte le verità saranno comprese quando le stesse si saranno derectus,'"* she said. "Do you know what it means?"

"It means 'All truths will be understood—'" Carina started.

"'When the stars align,'" Her Ladyship finished. "There are many ancient texts which reference the great treasure. And they, too, speak of the Map No Man Can Read."

"There are?" Carina asked, dismayed. She hadn't been aware of that.

"Indeed." Lady Devonshire nodded. "But none of them have suggested *how* to find the map. It seems Galileo was alone in that. Tell me, what do you think he meant?"

"I believe he meant the map is hidden in the stars," Carina answered.

"But *how* does one see it, then?" Lady Devonshire asked.

Carina shook her head. "I do not know."

Her Ladyship sighed. "It has been a long time since I have conversed about the heavens." Then she frowned. "Tell me, child, what do you want for your future?"

"I wish to study the stars," Carina said confidently.

"So you have not changed your mind?" Lady Devonshire asked.

At that, Carina paused. "Changed my mind? What do you mean?"

"I have told you that studying the stars is a fool's effort," Lady Devonshire stated. "I thought the opportunity of continued employment might have brought you to your senses."

Carina frowned. She didn't like where this was going. "Forgive me, my lady, but I thought you summoned me because of the notes. . . ."

"Yes, yes, they were quite persistent," Lady Devonshire replied. "And from them I gathered you would not let the matter drop. Tell me, if you will not see reason regarding your future, what do you suppose your father wanted?"

"That I should study the stars," Carina repeated. "And that I should find the Map No Man Can Read, which will lead to a great treasure. That is why he left me the book."

"Are you certain?" asked Lady Devonshire. "Perhaps he wanted to grant you some ease of life. The ruby on this book is valuable, after all."

Carina shook her head. "I am positive, my lady, he wanted me to study the stars."

Lady Devonshire closed the book. "I admire your persistence, but you are incorrect. Your father wanted something better for you. Lord Willoughby saw it, as well, and thought I could be of help. That is why I have made arrangements for you to train as a governess in London."

"A governess?" cried Carina, taken aback. "But, Your Ladyship—"

"There will be no argument," Lady Devonshire said matter-of-factly. "I am offering you a position in life that will be far more advanced than mere service work can ever allow. Surely you must be grateful?"

"It is not a matter of being grateful." Carina could not

hold her tongue any longer. "It is not my destiny to be a governess. I am meant to study the stars. Your Ladyship *must* see that."

"I do not," Lady Devonshire replied.

"But *you* did!" Carina said accusingly. "You studied the stars—you still can if you want! What happened here to make you turn away from it?"

Lady Devonshire's face grew cold. "That is not your concern."

"But it is!" exclaimed Carina. "I saw the observatory. You like having someone to discuss the heavens with. Why can't I be your student? You can teach me."

"Because you are young and foolish and do not know what you are asking," Lady Devonshire snapped.

"Then tell me!" Carina cried. "Tell me what it is that I am asking, because clearly you have done it, and I see no reason why I cannot do the same."

Anger flashed across Lady Devonshire's face. Carina knew she had far overstepped her bounds—again. She half expected Her Ladyship to dismiss her on the spot—again.

After a very, *very* long moment, Lady Devonshire stood.

"You will follow me," she said through tight lips. "And I will show you firsthand the ruin your life will become through such foolishness."

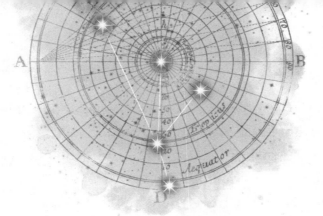

CHAPTER 16

THE CANDELABRA FLICKERED EERILY on the stone walls as Carina followed Lady Devonshire up the winding staircase to the observatory. The lady produced a large metal key ring from her pocket and opened the door with a heavy thunk.

Carina felt her heart quicken as they entered the observatory. It still seemed to her that the room held the answer to everything she had longed for her whole life. If she had the choice, she would never leave.

Lady Devonshire walked to a tall bookcase piled high with books, parchments, and charts. She ran her hand over the spines and papers as though choosing. Still holding the candelabra, she selected an overstuffed book filled with loose astronomical diagrams.

Lady Devonshire turned, and Carina held out her hands, expecting Her Ladyship to hand it to her.

Abruptly, Lady Devonshire threw it violently on the ground.

Papers scattered everywhere; charts fluttered about the legs of the observatory table and telescope.

Without a word, Lady Devonshire turned back to the bookcase and selected another collection of papers. She hurled them to the ground as well.

"What are you doing?" Carina exclaimed.

But Her Ladyship didn't respond. She turned back to the shelf over and over again, ripping books and papers from where they rested under thick layers of dust and strewing them about the observatory floor.

"Stop it!" Carina cried. "You'll ruin them!"

"They are already ruined!" yelled Lady Devonshire. Her wild look from that first evening had returned. "From the moment *he* died!"

She pointed to a painting on the wall Carina had not noticed. In the glow of the candelabra, Carina saw the portrait of an esteemed-looking man. He bore a striking resemblance to Lady Devonshire.

"My brother!" Lady Devonshire exclaimed. "Lord Devonshire. The finest astronomer to set foot upon English soil. For years we worked side by side, minding the heavens each night until the sun rose. Charting comets—cataloging countless stars. We made discoveries even the professors at the university had not. Saw things they had only dreamed of!"

With a violent heft, Lady Devonshire swiped away everything on the observatory table—loose charts, instruments, and inkwells. Debris scattered everywhere.

Carina involuntarily clutched her head. "You're breaking it all!"

But Lady Devonshire was a woman possessed. "Together, we stepped beyond what mankind thought possible!"

Crash. Lady Devonshire stormed across the room and swung at an astrolabe, which plummeted to the floor.

"We opened up the heavens!"

Smash. An armillary sphere splintered across the floor.

"They named stars after my brother. Awarded him the university's highest honor."

Smash, smash, smash. Compasses and quadrants flew to the ground.

"I knew that they would never recognize my contributions, that I would always be in the shadows. But as long as we worked together, it didn't seem to matter."

Lady Devonshire moved toward the telescope. Carina's eyes grew wide.

"Please, don't!" she cried, grabbing Lady Devonshire's sleeve.

The woman tried mightily to heave the candelabra at the telescope, but Carina used all her strength to hold her back. Finally, Lady Devonshire relented.

"And then he died," she said, her voice breaking. "And this—all of it—was suddenly out of reach."

Lady Devonshire seemed to shrink inward. Carina guided her to the table, and the woman sat down, burying her face in her hands.

"The university would no longer accept my contributions," Lady Devonshire continued. "They wouldn't even acknowledge that I had held any part in the discoveries my brother and I made together. Had he not left me everything, they would have tried to take away the instruments, too."

She dug her fingers into her hair. "I was not even allowed to mourn him at the memorial they held at the university. I was told by everyone it was not a woman's place."

Lady Devonshire grew quiet. Carina couldn't tell if she was crying.

Finally, the woman lifted her head to look at Carina. Her eyes were red, her expression haunted. "So you see, girl, *this* is what awaits you. Isolation. Ruin. The hand of God revealed to you in the stars only to be snatched away while you are told it was never yours to begin with."

Carina knelt down by the table. "Your Ladyship," she began hesitantly. "It is not gone. It is still there. I have been told all my life not to look to the stars, but they are there all the same. Just because people tell you that you can't study them doesn't mean you shouldn't."

Lady Devonshire shook her head. "I had everything, every possible means available to me, and it was all taken away because I am not a man. What more could you, as an orphan, ever hope to do? The world is not ours to control."

"But we don't need to control the world," Carina said. "Just the heavens."

Lady Devonshire looked at Carina, and then her gaze shifted down.

"This all means something," Carina continued, pointing to the charts scattered around the floor. "Something great. My father knew it, and though he left me nothing else in life, he left me this. You say it cannot offer me a life. *This* is all I have to live for. Please, you are the only one who can teach me to study the stars. I want to learn from you. We can work together, and you can study the stars once more." She paused. "Will you teach me?"

Lady Devonshire stayed still and silent. Carina wondered if the woman would begin shouting at her again. After a long while, she began to wonder if Lady Devonshire had even heard her question.

But then a faint glimmer came to Lady Devonshire's eye. She looked out the window, up at the stars, and remained like that for a long, long time.

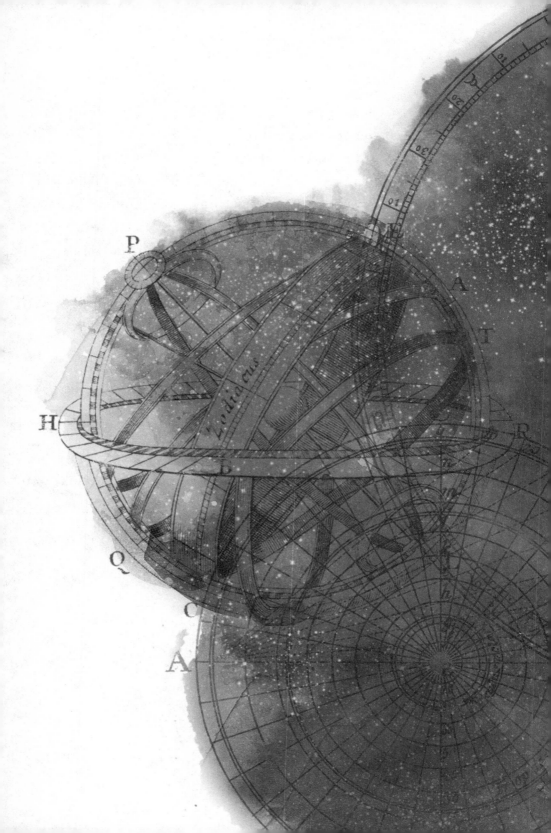

PART THREE
MINDING THE HEAVENS

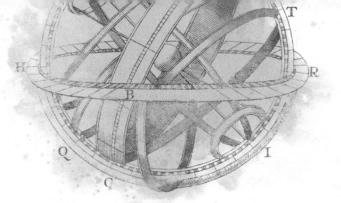

CHAPTER 17

"LONGITUDE TWO DEGREES NORTH." Carina stared intently through the telescope eyepiece.

"Two degrees north seems two too much," Lady Devonshire replied. She wrote down the adjustment on a chart in front of her.

"No, it is correct." Carina smiled. "It is only too much if we do not get the two we are looking for."

Carina adjusted the telescope and returned to the eyepiece.

"There, there it is!" she cried. "Twin stars! I told you!"

Lady Devonshire stepped forward and gazed through the eyepiece herself.

"Upon my word," she said. "This is extraordinary."

"Another entry for the catalog?" Carina asked excitedly.

Lady Devonshire nodded. "It would appear so. That brings us to"—she did a quick calculation—"over two hundred, does it not?"

Carina beamed.

She had been studying astronomy with Lady Devonshire for the past four years. Since that night in the observatory, everything had changed. Carina had become a sort of ward of Her Ladyship, with her own room at the estate.

It hadn't been an easy adjustment at first. Lady Devonshire had her own way of observing the stars—a precise method that involved *her* doing the observing and *Carina's* doing the recording. Carina wouldn't have minded if she had been given responsibilities other than simply being Lady Devonshire's scribe. She yearned for the opportunity to gaze through the telescope herself.

It was only when Lady Devonshire fell slightly ill during one especially cold winter that things had turned around. Her Ladyship had felt too weak to climb up to the observatory, giving Carina the opportunity to "mind the heavens" alone, observing and recording late into the night. And when Carina had discovered a comet passing by in close orbit to Earth, Lady Devonshire had been in such disbelief that she'd dragged herself from her sickbed to see it in person. Though the woman never admitted it, Carina could tell that from that moment on, Her Ladyship had a newfound respect for Carina's abilities. She'd even agreed to teach Carina horology, the study of time. It was more than Carina could have dared to hope for.

Naturally, things had been tense with the servants at first. Celia would curtsy awkwardly if she passed Carina in the halls, and Mrs. Rossi refused to look at her altogether. But after a while, Celia started to feel comfortable responding to Carina's warm greetings, and most of the others either moved on to new positions or stopped talking about how Carina had once been a servant at the estate. The truth was now that Her Ladyship was happier, everyone was happier. Light had been restored to Hanover Hall.

Carina's nineteenth birthday was approaching, and she had to imagine she was one of the youngest astronomers in the country to have cataloged so many new stars. Perhaps one of the youngest in the world.

"Who do you suppose the university will attribute this discovery to?" Carina asked as she blotted the freshly inked chart and prepared an envelope for the morning delivery.

"Who can say?" Lady Devonshire leaned back, rubbing her eyes. "It seems to be someone different each time. But they know it is us."

"Does it ever bother you?" Carina asked. "That we do all the work and they get all the credit?"

Lady Devonshire smiled. "Perhaps it should. But as a very

wise pupil once told me, we need not control the world." She patted the telescope. "Just the heavens."

* * *

The next morning, Carina took the carriage from Hanover Hall to the nearby university. One of the students waited outside for the usual Monday-morning delivery.

"What news from the stars?" he asked brightly as Carina hopped down from the carriage.

"You'll need to read to find out," she said, handing him the chart in the envelope.

The student shook his head. "When will you and Lady Devonshire ever claim ownership of all the work you do?"

"When the world stops referring to women of science as witches," she said.

"Well, for the record, they know where these charts come from." The student tapped the envelope on his head for emphasis. "They are simply too stubborn to admit it."

"Then thank heavens for messengers like you." Carina smiled. "Besides, the real treasure lies not in single stars, but in the patterns that can be derived from them."

"What do you mean?" the student asked, curiosity piqued.

"That is a mystery for another time," Carina said, heading back toward the carriage. "One hopefully soon to be solved. Take care. There will be more next week!"

Carina waved as the carriage pulled away. But a commotion at the corner of the university caught her attention.

"Driver, please hold for a moment," she called.

Carina looked out the window. A group of young men, all students at the university, were gathered around a sign attached to the wall.

"Please wait for me. I will be right back," Carina instructed the driver.

Quickly, she hopped back down and hurried to where the crowd was gathered.

Carina tried to peer over the students' heads, but there were too many of them blocking her view for her to read the sign properly.

"What is this all about?" Carina asked.

A tall student stared down at her. "Nothing to concern yourself with, girl," he said. "Move along."

Carina huffed and stood up a little straighter. "You dare speak to the daughter of the university dean in that manner?"

"The daughter of the—I'm—I'm so sorry, miss. I didn't realize the dean had a daughter," the tall student stammered.

"Tell me your name," Carina demanded.

The student sputtered. "I'm—I'm no one of importance."

"On that we can agree," she said. "Now help me get a look at that sign before I change my mind and report you to my father."

"Of course, miss," the student said. "Stand back! Stand back, everyone! The dean's daughter wishes to see!"

The sea of students parted and Carina stepped forward to read the sign.

LEGENDS OF THE HEAVENS

A DISCOURSE ON MYTHS, MAPS, AND BLOOD MOONS

FROM STUDIES PERFORMED IN THE CARIBBEAN

CHARLES SWIFT, SON OF GEORGE SWIFT, ESQ.,

TO PRESENT SATURDAY AFTERNOON

"Myths, maps, and blood moons . . ." Carina mouthed to herself. She and Lady Devonshire had recently been charting blood moons. There were indicators in the diary that pointed to their being significant in locating the map.

"Where is this talk to be presented?" she asked a short student nearby.

"At the university, miss," he said. "In the great hall."

"Indeed," Carina said quietly as the student moved along. She studied the sign with keen interest. "Then I suppose that is where I must be."

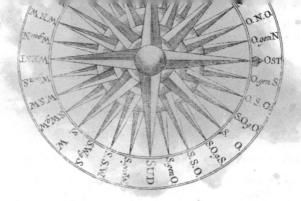

CHAPTER 18

"ABSOLUTELY NOT."

Lady Devonshire paced angrily as Carina stood pleading her case in the observatory.

"But the man presenting this discourse has traveled all the way from the islands," Carina insisted. "Perhaps there is something in his lecture we can learn from. Something we have overlooked."

"Carina Smyth, we have discussed this before," Lady Devonshire said sharply. "I am not your mother—I will not pretend to be. But how many times must we have this argument? As a woman, you are not allowed at the university discourses. I nearly risked my estate to rescue you the last foolhardy time you snuck in dressed as a boy. And you nearly risked the stockade. I will not put my life's work on the line every time you want to go off and hear a lecture."

Carina knew what Lady Devonshire was referring to. The previous year, she had desperately wanted to attend a university discourse about newly discovered planetary satellites. Naturally, women were forbidden to attend. But that hadn't stopped Carina. All she'd needed was a jacket. And pants. And a strategically combed wig. She would have made it to the end of the lecture without getting spotted, too, if she hadn't been compelled to raise her hand and ask a question. (And really, who could blame her? The professor giving the lecture had made a clear misstatement regarding the Galilean moons.) But the ensuing riot had involved guards in pursuit, a trampled wig, and many, *many* stern lectures from Lady Devonshire, complete with threats of sending Carina away.

Still, this discourse was different. This one could help them find the *map*!

"Lady Devonshire, please," Carina begged. "We have spoon-fed the university over two hundred stars. Surely they owe us a favor."

"My dear child, by now you should know life offers us no favors." Lady Devonshire frowned. "Much less the university faculty."

"But . . . it's a lecture about blood moons," Carina insisted.

"This could be it—the clue that helps us find the map and the Trident of Poseidon!"

Lady Devonshire sighed heavily. "Carina, of late you have become more and more obsessed with finding the Trident and less so with minding the heavens. Do you still wish to study the stars?"

"Of course!" exclaimed Carina.

"Then focus on the science," said Lady Devonshire. "The map is a legend. Galileo himself was uncertain of its existence. Our search is for truth, not for treasure."

Carina was about to retort, but for once, she held her tongue. Over the past four years, she'd learned that their attitudes toward finding the Map No Man Can Read were very different from each other. Carina felt that searching for the map *was* scientific. The mere fact that it led to a legendary treasure did not make it any less worthy of pursuit. Even the fact that Earth orbited the sun had been considered myth not all that long before. The map could be found through science; Carina was certain of it.

Lady Devonshire, however, did not feel the same way.

"But," Carina pleaded weakly, "it's *blood moons*."

"Promise me you will not attempt to sneak in," Lady Devonshire directed. "Do I have your word?"

Carina nodded begrudgingly. "I promise."

* * *

Carina broke her promise.

That Saturday, the comb-over wig made a reappearance, along with a spare university uniform and jacket.

Carina disliked going against Lady Devonshire. But she just couldn't stay away from a discourse on something that could possibly open up new doors in their search. It would be foolish not to attend, even unscientific. She was sure Lady Devonshire would understand once Carina came back with new findings.

The crowd for the lecture was unusually large. Carina had no difficulty blending in. If there was one thing she had learned about university students, it was that they were all extremely self-absorbed. Short of something unusual (like a student in a comb-over wig challenging the professor about the Galilean moons), they couldn't be bothered with anything that didn't directly impact them or their studies.

A distinguished-looking man in naval attire approached the lectern. He was young, Carina noted. Probably not more than twenty-five. His uniform was polished and his skin tan. Except for an unruly mop of brown hair, everything about his appearance was impressive.

"Greetings," he said, opening his discourse. "My name is Charles Swift, and I've traveled here today from the island of Saint Martin in the Caribbean. My father is G. W. Swift, Esquire, the owner of Swift and Sons Chart House there. I have spent some time in the Caribbean and amassed a good amount of knowledge on the connection between local lore, legend, and the applied science of astronomy. It is upon those topics I'd like to focus our discourse today."

Carina listened with fascination as Charles Swift discussed the study of astronomy on the islands. She was amazed at how much of it seemed rooted in legend and folklore: myths of the stars' effect on people's actions; tales of celestial events guiding sailors to their demise; even overarching fear of witchcraft.

How absurd! she thought. *Do the people there really believe this nonsense?*

To his credit, Charles Swift did not seem particularly swayed by the supernatural implications of astronomy. But then again, he didn't seem to refute them, either. . . .

"Which brings us to our discussion of blood moons," he said suddenly.

Carina perked up. That was what she had been waiting for.

"Now, the blood moon, of course, is caused by the earth's shadow falling across the moon during an eclipse, giving it a bloodred color," he explained. "Though to the more superstitious on the islands, a moon tinged red is the harbinger of death and destruction. Others believe it is all-revealing, akin to the mythical third eye. There is even a saying on the islands that 'all truths shall be revealed in the light of a blood moon.'"

"All truths . . ." Carina mouthed. Those were nearly

Galileo's exact words. That couldn't be a coincidence! *Perhaps the light of a blood moon is what will allow the map to be seen in the stars!* she realized.

Carina could barely contain her excitement. She waited until the end of the lecture, after the student body had applauded politely, to make her move. Quickly, she slipped through the crowd up to Charles Swift.

"Excuse me," she said in as deep a voice as she could muster. "I just had to tell you, I found your talk fascinating."

"Thank you," Charles said rather offhandedly. "The islands are a fascinating place."

"I'm particularly intrigued by your discourse on blood moons," Carina continued. "These are rare occurrences, you say?"

"Indeed," Charles replied, packing up his papers and parchments. "Though one of the largest blood moons is predicted to be visible on the islands in just a few months. My return ship sails next week. If the winds are in our favor, we will be back in time to see it."

"A few months . . ." Carina breathed. "Fascinating."

Just then, a student bumped into her back.

"Hey!" Carina yelped in her normal voice. Charles gave her a look, and she composed herself. "I mean, hey," she said more deeply.

A strange look crossed Charles's face. "Is . . . is there something wrong with your hair?"

"My hair?" Carina asked, reaching up. She gasped. Her wig was out of alignment.

"Oh, uh, no, no, just a mild condition." She adjusted the wig quickly. "You know . . . not enough sun and all."

Charles Swift furrowed his brow. "I have been to the university many times, but I have not seen you before," he said.

Carina noted with alarm that some of the other professors had noticed her speaking with Charles, and they, too, were clearly trying to place who she was.

"I, uh, am new," she said quickly. "Thank you again—splendid discourse! Much accolade, a pleasure to meet you . . . I have to go."

Carina turned to hurry off, but not before Charles offered some parting words.

"May the stars always guide you home," he said.

Carina stopped dead in her tracks.

"What did you say?" she asked, turning.

Charles looked up in surprise. "Oh, my apologies. It's just a phrase from a Saint Martin children's song. I'm afraid some habits never cease."

"A children's song?" Carina repeated. A distant memory had been jogged at the back of her mind . . . one she hadn't thought of in years.

"Yes," said Charles. He mulled over the lyrics to the song for a moment.

"With the sea at your back and the wind in your sails,
though you be far from shore, you are never alone.
Simply look north, Carina prevails.
May the stars always shine and guide you toward home."

Carina was speechless. That song . . . that was the song that appeared in some of her haziest, earliest memories.

"The children of Saint Martin sing that?" she asked.

Charles nodded, snapping his bag shut. "Yes, though Saint Martin is a busy port. People come and go from all corners of the world. I suppose the song could be from any-where. It's been many years since I've sung it myself. But that one phrase has always stuck with me."

Carina's mind raced. She had been aboard boats, and she remembered hearing that song as a child. Did that mean she had once lived in . . .

"I need to get to Saint Martin," she said under her breath. All paths, all celestial events, all stars led there.

A nearby professor pointed toward Carina. His compan-ion stepped forward.

It was time to go.

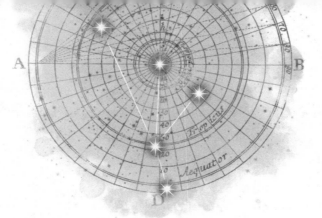

CHAPTER 19

"YOU DISOBEYED MY DIRECT ORDERS!" Lady Devonshire was furious. "You could easily have been spotted and everything we have worked toward would have come to an end. *Again.*"

"But don't you see?" Carina argued. The setting sun glared red through the observatory windows. "The key to everything lies in Saint Martin. We must travel there. The blood moon will be visible in a few months' time. Saint Martin is where we will find the clues we need to read the map and locate the treasure!"

"Carina, I grow tired of explaining the nature of our

work to you." Lady Devonshire pressed her temples. "We are scientists. We are *not* treasure hunters."

"But Galileo was both!" exclaimed Carina. "Why do they need to be separate?"

"Because one is rational and the other is a fool's quest!" yelled Lady Devonshire. "Have you learned so little that you are still a child in this line of thinking?"

Carina winced. That stung. Lady Devonshire knew her better than that.

"Have I not learned everything I know from *you*?" Carina shot back. "We are on a quest for the truth. What makes this any different? There is an astronomical mystery to be solved and we are the only ones with the tools to solve it." She thought of the diary. Somehow she knew that finding the truth was what her father would have wanted. She needed Lady Devonshire to understand that. "What is the point of learning without *applying* that knowledge to anything? Have you been locked up in this hall so long that you are afraid to venture out into the unknown?"

Lady Devonshire's face grew tight.

Uh-oh, Carina thought. She knew that look. All further argument was about to be shut down in three . . . two . . . one . . .

"This discussion is over," Lady Devonshire said firmly. "You have allowed your emotions to get the best of you. You believe that finding your treasure will bring you to your father. It will not. He abandoned you, and there is nothing to be gained from this fool's quest but regret. Perhaps if you do not understand that by now, then you are not capable of learning it."

Lady Devonshire sat down at her desk and began writing. "You will meet me in my sitting room tomorrow morning to discuss your future."

Carina sucked in her breath. "What do you mean?"

"You are nearly nineteen years old." Lady Devonshire appeared to be writing a letter. "You are now of the age when it is crucial to determine permanent establishment. You cannot remain at Hanover Hall indefinitely. It is time we find a path suited to your talents."

"Suited to my . . ." Carina started. Her temper bubbled over. "We have one disagreement, and you decide to send me away? What kind of arrangement is that?"

"One that I believe indicates how deeply invested I am in you." Lady Devonshire sealed her letter with a wax stamp. Carina could read the address on the front; it was to Lord Willoughby. "I only desire what is best for your future."

Carina set her jaw. "With all due respect, I do not believe you know what that is anymore."

* * *

Later that night, in her room, Carina looked through the window at the stars. The sky was clear and the moon dark, allowing the distant bursts of light to twinkle at their brightest.

They blurred in Carina's vision. She knew she had Lady Devonshire to thank for nearly everything she had accomplished in studying the stars. But this—this was too much. How could Her Ladyship not see how crucial traveling to Saint Martin was? How important it was, if not to science, then to her?

Carina sniffled and brushed away her tears. She knew what she had to do, but for one of the rare times in her life, she was hesitant to move forward.

If I go, I will be on my own again, she thought miserably.

The truth was Carina had grown fond of Hanover Hall. And of Lady Devonshire. The woman wasn't particularly warm. But it had been nice to feel like she belonged— somewhere.

"But this isn't my home," Carina said to herself grimly. "And my destiny lies across the sea."

Carina gazed around her room—at the nice furniture and the well-made dresses peeking out of the armoire. Perhaps while she had sought clarity at Hanover Hall, her true path had been obscured. Her quest was not just for science, but for the truth—the truth of who she was, and of her birthright.

"Lady Devonshire is right. I cannot stay at Hanover Hall. It is time for me to follow my destiny."

Quietly, Carina moved to the writing desk at the corner of her room and pulled out a sheet of paper. Her hand shook as she penned the letter. But she needed Her Ladyship to understand, at least somewhat. The woman would likely not believe her thanks. But maybe she would with time. And who could say? Perhaps Carina would be back one day.

She signed the letter the way that seemed most fitting:

May the stars always guide you,
Carina

Then Carina got to work. She stuffed her most important belongings into a travel bag—just enough that she would not be weighed down. Of course, the diary rested in her satchel at her side.

In the darkness of the estate halls, Carina slipped toward the sitting room and placed her letter under the door. Lady Devonshire would receive it in the morning with her tea.

Carina shuddered. There was finality to placing that letter under the door. And there was no turning back.

She had a ship to catch.

* * *

Several weeks later, a lone vessel crashed through the waves over the Atlantic. Sea-foam splashed, spraying the deck at the bow with mist. It was nighttime, and the full moon dipped in and out of sight among long clouds, casting eerie shadows on the deck of the ship.

Only one shadow was out of place.

Carina stepped up to the bow, looking out over the ocean. A cloak was wrapped tightly around her shoulders, and she wore a hat pulled down low over her forehead.

In the satchel she clutched by her side was the diary. She pressed her hand to it and could swear she felt warmth emanating from the ruby through the satchel's fabric. A comforting warmth, like a beacon in the night.

Carina gazed out at the shadowy sea before her and smiled.

She was sailing to Saint Martin—and to her destiny.

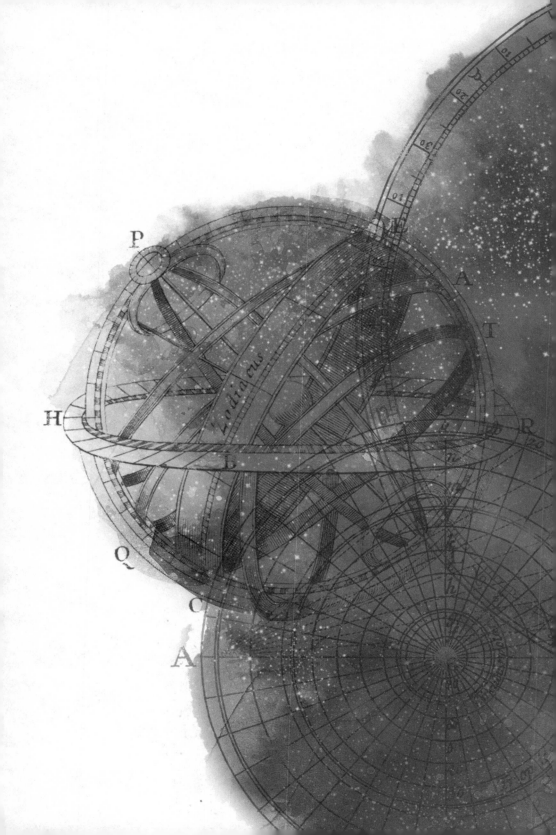

Part Four

THE CARIBBEAN

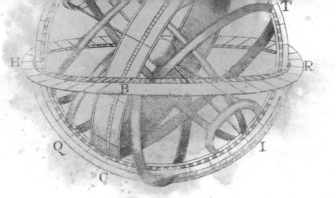

CHAPTER 20

"CARINA SMYTH, YOU ARE AN ORPHAN BORN OF the devil—accused of practicing witchcraft! Before you die, do you have anything to confess?"

The elderly priest stared down his nose at the girl behind bars. Carina grasped the cell gate tightly, her hands wavering near the lock.

"I confess that I am not a witch," she said, her eyes steely. "That I am a woman of science. I confess that I have survived on my own, with nothing but a diary from a father I never met and a quest for the truth of who I am. I confess that I will die before I give up this search. And I confess that while we have been talking, I have picked this lock."

Carina flung open the cell door and ran for her life.

Stunned, the priest stood with his mouth gaping before finally coming to his senses. "Stop! Witch!"

Carina bolted up the stone steps of the crumbling prison cell and out into the busy village streets.

She was definitely *not* in England anymore.

Coaches with sun canopies rumbled past, kicking up dust in the sandy streets. Naval officers patrolled the main stretch, gold uniform buttons glinting in the light. Genteel women carrying parasols perused the shops and shielded themselves from the glare of the sun.

Stretched out before Carina was a bustling, thriving island town teeming with enterprise and people *far* too busy to notice the nineteen-year-old girl in the tattered dress with a chain dangling from her wrist.

This was the Caribbean island of Saint Martin.

Carina looked sharply from left to right. She needed to find a way to blend in, and fast. She had been on Saint Martin for several weeks, and though the island itself provided an idyllic backdrop of palm trees and tranquility, the people there did not match it.

When Carina had arrived, the first thing she'd done was ask a soldier for directions to Swift and Sons Chart House. The soldier had scoffed. What business did a *girl* have looking for Swift and Sons Chart House? So Carina had calmly stated that she was a woman of science and had spent her life studying the stars.

That was her first mistake.

Her second was to assume that the people there couldn't possibly be superstitious enough to sentence her to *hanging* for witchcraft.

They were.

After weeks of dodging and hiding, having skirmishes with the local authorities, and eventually being caught and tried, Carina was running out of time. The blood moon was fast approaching, and if she was going to do what she had come to Saint Martin to do, it was now or never.

But first she needed to escape.

Carina ran straight for a thick crowd of people gathering in the center of the town square. Two soldiers were hot on her trail.

"Stop that witch!" one of the soldiers cried behind her.

Luckily, there was too much commotion for anyone to hear them. Everyone in Saint Martin had turned up for the unveiling of the new Royal Bank, promised to be "the most secure banking institution in the Caribbean."

Carina bobbed and weaved among men and women, smacking into elbows and parasols. The two soldiers chasing her were losing ground. She was about to zip out from the crowd and into an alleyway when . . .

"Stop right there!"

A young soldier nervously blocked her path. He was either new to patrol or actually afraid of Carina's "witchcraft" abilities.

Without missing a beat, Carina spun around him and ducked under a nearby wagon. The soldier blinked. He had not even seen where she'd gone. Carina crawled under the wagon and popped out on the other side.

By that point, the two other guards had caught up with the young soldier. They panted for breath and looked this way and that. But Carina was nowhere to be seen.

Carina watched from behind the wagon as the officers turned and came face to face with their superior, Lieutenant John Scarfield.

"I—I'm sorry, sir," one of the officers stammered. "That witch escaped her chains."

Scarfield's face turned blistering red. "You're telling me"—Scarfield grabbed the soldier by his shirtfront—"that four of my men have lost one girl? Perhaps this is why I was denied a fleet of my own, why I'm docked in Saint Martin instead of fighting wars in West Africa!"

Scarfield angrily threw the soldier to the ground.

"The navy sent me here to kill witches," Scarfield said with disgust. "Now find me that wicked lass, or you'll swing in her place!"

The soldiers saluted and scurried off, back into the crowd.

Meanwhile, from her vantage point behind the wagon, Carina panted as she caught her breath. When she had set sail for Saint Martin, she never expected to encounter that. How blind were those men, that their sole duty was to search for witches? It seemed to Carina that their job was more to control the population through fear.

Still, they meant business, and the last call had been too close.

Carina had her own business to take care of.

It was time to pay Swift and Sons Chart House a visit.

CHAPTER 21

SWIFT AND SONS CHART HOUSE was a small shop, tucked in the back corner of a cobblestone street. For the most part, it looked like an ordinary store. Just a typical building facade with tall windows and a green-painted door. However, Carina knew it was the right place by the large golden telescope protruding from the back of the building— that and the crude sign tacked to the front.

SWIFT AND SONS CHART HOUSE

NO DOGS OR WOMEN ALLOWED

Carina ignored the sign as she quietly slipped inside. Compared to the town square, the chart house was deliciously quiet. Clocks and chronometers ticked softly, marking the time, and astronomical diagrams and ship's logs were piled all the way to the ceiling.

Carina gazed around in awe. Aside from Lady Devonshire's observatory, this was the largest room dedicated to astronomy Carina had ever seen. And in the corner of the room stood a majestic contraption, still one of the most marvelous things in the world, to Carina's mind: a telescope, situated by the window to face toward the heavens.

Carina approached it with great regard. But when she looked through the eyepiece, Carina frowned. Something was wrong.

The celestial fix was off by at least two degrees! To the untrained eye, it was only a slight discrepancy. But to an astronomer . . .

Carina glanced up at the maps on the walls, disappointed.

To an astronomer, it could mean a lifetime of work. How could the senior Mr. Swift never have noticed?

She had begun tinkering with the telescope's mechanism when footsteps echoed behind her.

"No *woman* has ever handled my telescope!" someone cried angrily.

Carina whirled around to find G. W. Swift, Esquire, the owner of the chart house, standing in the doorway. He was a short man with a white powdered wig and dark arched eyebrows. He was not nearly as esteemed-looking as his son, Carina noted. But then again, she had never seen the younger Swift when he was angry.

"Sir, your celestial fix was off," Carina explained. "I've adjusted two degrees north. Your maps will no longer be imprecise. Though you will have to start over with these." She motioned to the maps framed along the walls of the chart house.

Mr. Swift stared at Carina incredulously. That was when he spotted the chain dangling from her wrist.

"You're a witch!" he sputtered.

"Sir, I am no witch," Carina replied, annoyed. Whatever hope she'd had that Swift would be as learned as his son had quickly disintegrated. "I simply made application to study astronomy at the university—"

"You *what*?" he exclaimed.

"Am I a witch for having cataloged two hundred stars?" she asked indignantly.

"*Witch!*" Mr. Swift repeated.

Carina was growing exasperated. She could feel her temper getting the best of her. Perhaps money would speak louder than reasoning.

"There is a blood moon coming," Carina said shortly. "I simply need to purchase a chronometer. I'll pay you double for selling to a woman."

She held up a chronometer and several gold coins. Surely the man would not pass up the opportunity for quick money.

But to her surprise, Mr. Swift shakily pulled out a pistol.

"Help!" he cried, nervously aiming the gun at Carina. "There's a witch in my shop!"

Carina gasped. He was going to shoot her!

Carina was about to dodge when, suddenly, a wild, dirty long-haired man toppled into the store.

She had only a second to take in his appearance, but that was all Carina needed. The man's eyes were blackened with kohl about the rims, and his hands were adorned with countless tattoos and rings. He wore a dusty tricornered hat askew atop his head, and a beaded braid of matted hair coiled down his shoulder. From the man's tattered captain's coat and gold teeth and the bottle of rum in his hand, Carina quickly pieced together what he was, which was quickly confirmed by Mr. Swift.

"A pirate!" he screamed. "There's a witch and a pirate in my store!"

The pirate looked around, eyeing Carina, Mr. Swift, and then the wall behind them.

"And a bank," he pointed out calmly.

Before Carina knew what was happening, the pirate grabbed her by the arm and pulled her away just as an enormous object crashed through the chart house walls, splitting the store in two.

Carina watched in shock as the entire store was demolished. Charts, globes, logs—everything went flying. But the pirate didn't allow her to stand for long. He dragged her along, and she gripped the chronometer tightly. Together, they began running.

Carina and the pirate sprinted through the streets, dodging legions of guards and soldiers, before dipping down a shadowed alleyway.

"It would seem you've brought the entire British army upon our heads!" Carina hissed.

"You appear to be popular with them, too," the pirate replied.

Carina huffed. To be sure, this man had a swagger about him, as though he knew exactly what he was doing. She glanced down at the half-empty bottle of rum in his hand. No, it looked like it was up to her to find them a hiding place—and fast!

"Come on, this way!" she hissed.

A few moments later, a band of guards hurried down the alley. They didn't even notice the two heads poking up like mannequins behind a line of formal dresses outside a tailor's shop.

The pirate looked sideways at Carina and frowned.

"Were you part of the plan?" he asked.

Carina had no idea what "plan" he was talking about, but if it involved more soldiers chasing her, she was not interested. "I'm not looking for trouble."

The pirate pulled a face of disgust. "What a horrible way to live."

"I need to escape," Carina said matter-of-factly. "Can you help me?" She wished there were somebody—anybody—else she could ask, but she found herself in a desperate situation.

The pirate mulled this over for a moment. "That man called you a witch. And witches are bad luck at sea."

Carina groaned. Was everyone on Saint Martin so daft that all they could think of were witches?

"We're not at sea," she said.

"Good point," the man replied. "But I am a pirate."

"But I am clearly not a witch," Carina whispered through gritted teeth.

"One of us is very confused," the pirate said.

"By all appraisals, that would be you," Carina retorted.

Suddenly, the sound of more footsteps thundered down the alleyway. It was Scarfield and his men. They had spotted them!

Carina held her breath. It looked like they were done for.

"Jack Sparrow!" yelled one of the guards as they approached.

"Would you excuse me?" the pirate, who appeared to be called Jack Sparrow, said to the soldiers. "I seem to have misplaced a bank."

With that, he grabbed Carina's hand and they raced away just as the soldiers opened fire. They ducked and dove past whizzing bullets, slamming hard into the entrance to a narrow staircase leading to the building rooftops. Without hesitating, Carina and Jack rushed up, up, up, stopping only when they reached the edge of the rooftop overlooking the alleys below.

"We're trapped!" Carina cried frantically. "What do we do?"

"You need to scream," Jack said.

Carina realized what was about to happen a split second too late. She gasped as Jack Sparrow shoved her—right off the rooftop.

Carina screamed. She was falling to her death!

THWOOMP!

In a giant poof of dust, she stopped. She had landed in a hay wagon rumbling along the street. Carina looked up in fury at the figure of the pirate, slowly getting smaller and smaller.

"Filthy pirate!" Carina shrieked.

But she didn't have time to waste on being furious. The guards had heard her scream and were closing in. She needed to find another escape route, or she would be captured again. And she was certain that this time they would make her chains pick-proof.

Carina looked left and right. *A distraction . . . a distraction . . . I need a distraction!*

Then she saw it—another wagon bumping down the narrow road, about to pass them.

She had only one shot; she'd need to time it perfectly.

With a swift kick, Carina slammed the back of her wagon open, releasing the rear loading ramp. Bushels and bushels of hay began tumbling into the street.

"Look out!" cried the soldiers, momentarily taken aback by the debris.

In that instant, Carina jumped over the sidewall and leaped into the wagon passing on the other side.

"Oof!" she cried, hitting the floor.

But her plan had worked. The guards were distracted enough that they hadn't noticed her switching rides.

Both the hay cart and the one she had jumped aboard screeched to a halt. Carina ducked down low. She heard both drivers hopping down to speak with the guards.

"Where is the witch?" screamed Scarfield, irately sifting through the hay covering the ground.

"She's vanished, sir!" said one of the soldiers. "An act of dark magic."

"These are bad times," another soldier commented. "First the boy washed ashore babbling of pirates and tridents. Now a witch capable of vanishing into thin air!"

"She may have shape-shifted!" another soldier exclaimed. "They can do that, you know. Transform into goats!"

"Into goats?" another soldier asked.

"Yes," the first soldier said grimly. "Nasty goats."

"Enough!" Scarfield kicked the hay. "I will have that witch's neck if it is the last thing I do."

Carina, meanwhile, barely dared to breath inside the wagon.

A boy washed ashore, babbling of pirates and *tridents*.

The timing couldn't be a coincidence. With the blood moon coming, perhaps this boy was also seeking the great treasure. There was no way of knowing for sure. But so far, she hadn't had much luck on her own. It would certainly be a relief to have some help on her quest.

If such a boy was on the island, she needed to find him.

The blood moon would arrive that night.

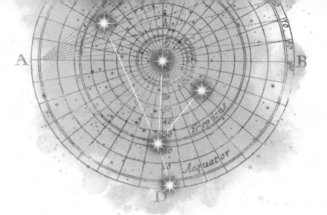

CHAPTER 22

CARINA SCRUBBED THE FLOORS VIGOROUSLY. All around her, soldiers and nuns passed this way and that, carrying bottles, salves, and bandages. An elderly nun approached the bed just behind Carina and placed a hand on the forehead of the young man who rested there.

"Alas, poor Henry Turner," the nun whispered. "I will pray for you."

Though Henry was asleep, his hands were shackled to the bed rails. Carina noted his appearance. He couldn't be much older than she was. His hands and face were covered with scrapes and bruises, and his forehead shone with fever. Still, Carina thought he was handsome. Tall, with skin tanned from the sun. And his light brown hair was swept back in a loose tie away from his chiseled features.

Carina pulled awkwardly at the neckline of her habit—part of her disguise as a nun. "This definitely does not suit me," she muttered.

But she supposed it was the only way to speak to the young man who might be able to help her.

It hadn't been hard to find him. Practically the whole town was talking about the mad soldier—the news of a ship gone down at sea and the sole survivor washed ashore, talking wildly of pirates and ghosts and tridents. Apparently, the only news that traveled faster in Saint Martin than stories of witchcraft was tales of the supernatural at sea.

But the whole town was also still buzzing with news of her: a young escaped witch with piercing blue eyes and the tongue of the devil. Carina had needed a disguise.

Suddenly, three soldiers marched into the hospital. Carina turned away. It was Lieutenant Scarfield, along with two burly soldiers.

Scarfield strode up to the young man's bedside and gave him a rough shake.

"The whole town speaks of you," Scarfield announced as Henry moaned, opening his eyes. "The only survivor of the *Monarch*—a boy who paddled all the way to Saint Martin on a piece of driftwood."

Henry tried to sit up, but the restraints held him back.

"Sir, let me go of these chains," Henry rasped, his voice dry. "I have to find Captain Jack Sparrow."

Scarfield scoffed. "It's my job to protect this island and these waters. Your sleeves have been ripped. The mark of treason!"

"We were attacked by the dead, sir," Henry insisted. "I tried to warn them!"

"You are a coward who ran from battle," Scarfield said. "And that is how you'll die."

Henry groaned and fell back to the bed, which elicited laughter from Scarfield and his men. As soon as the soldiers had stepped away, Carina hurried to the bedside.

"I don't believe you're a coward," she said, handing him some water.

Henry took the water and drank eagerly. But as soon as he had finished, he turned away. "Please leave me, Sister," he said.

Carina huffed. "I've risked my life to come here. To see if you truly believe as I believe—that the Trident will be found."

At that, Henry's eyes focused on Carina, and he saw her for the first time.

"Tell me why you seek the Trident," Carina said, pressing him.

"The Trident can break any curse at sea," Henry explained. "My father is trapped by such a curse."

Carina frowned. She had hoped the boy would be a scholar of science, like her. Not a simple fool like the rest of the people on this bloody island. Was everyone there so blindly superstitious? Considering Mr. Swift, Henry, and the authorities trying to hang her, Carina was beginning to worry that traveling to Saint Martin had been a mistake.

"You're aware of the fact that curses are not supported by science?" she asked.

"Neither are ghosts," Henry replied.

Carina sighed. "So you *have* gone mad. The laws of modern science—"

"Have nothing to do with the myths of the sea!" Henry interrupted.

Carina stood to leave. "I should never have come here."

The young man grasped her wrist. "Then why did you?"

"I need to get off this island," Carina said, "to solve the Map—"

"No Man Can Read," Henry finished for her. "Left behind by Poseidon himself."

Carina stared at him, wide-eyed. Perhaps there was more to the young man than met the eye. "So you have read the ancient texts?"

"In each language they were written," Henry replied. "And no man has ever seen this map."

Carina smiled. "Luckily, I am a woman."

Carefully, she withdrew Galileo's diary from her nun's habit.

"This is the diary of Galileo Galilei," she explained. "He spent his life looking for the map. This is why he invented the spyglass. Why astronomers have spent their lives looking to the sky."

Henry watched as she opened to the drawing of a cluster of five stars above the sea. "You're saying the Map No Man Can Read is hidden in the stars?" he asked.

"Yes," Carina answered. "But I have yet to see it."

"Just because you can't see something doesn't mean it's not there," Henry said.

Carina stared at him. Even though he might be mad, she had the strangest feeling that for the first time, someone truly understood her quest. And she couldn't help being impressed by his dedication to reading the ancient texts.

"The diary was left to me by my father." The words tumbled out of her mouth. "He believed I could find what no man has ever found, and I will not let him down. Soon there will be a blood moon. Only then will the map be read and the Trident found."

Henry gazed at her long and hard. He, too, seemed to feel like he was being understood for the first time.

"Who are you?" he asked, his tone one of quiet wonder.

An angry voice pierced the quiet of the hospital. *"Carina Smyth!"*

It was Scarfield. Carina had been spotted.

Dread washed over her. There was no way to escape this time; they had her cornered.

Desperately, she slipped a small metal pick from her sleeve into Henry's shackle lock.

"If you wish to save your father, you'll have to save me," she whispered urgently. "Find us a ship, and the Trident will be ours."

"Turn to me, witch!" Scarfield commanded.

Without another word, Carina took off running. She crashed into nuns and leaped over beds, but Scarfield's men were on her in a second. They pinned her down before the chase had even begun.

"Sir, he's gone!" one of the soldiers suddenly cried out.

Scarfield whipped to face Henry Turner's hospital bed. It was empty, the loose shackles piled in a heap.

Carina panted, catching her breath.

Henry Turner was her only hope now.

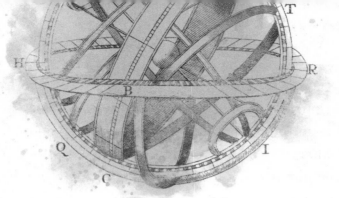

CHAPTER 23

LATER THAT NIGHT, Carina was making calculations on the wall of her dingy jail cell, the only light coming from the cloudy night sky through the tiny window.

She finished the equation she was working on and took a step away, peering back and forth between her figures and diagrams and the ones in the diary.

What am I missing? she asked herself in frustration. She had come to the Caribbean for answers, and she was no closer to figuring out the map than she had been in England. And now she was imprisoned, to boot. She wondered what Lady Devonshire would have had to say about her present situation.

Sighing, Carina glanced around the gray cell, her eyes

resting on the chronometer next to her. Miraculously, neither the chronometer nor the diary had been confiscated by the soldiers when she'd been captured. The only thing they seemed intent on was her hanging—which she supposed was enough.

Outside, a cloud shifted and moonlight poured into the cell. *The blood moon,* Carina thought. And then another light caught her eye. Quickly turning the diary over, Carina saw that the ruby was *glowing*.

"Just because you can't see something doesn't mean it's not there," Carina breathed. She plucked the ruby from the cover of the diary and angled it so the moon's light shone directly through, illuminating the entire diary cover.

She gasped.

A message was written on the cover of the diary, visible only in the light of the blood moon!

"'To release the power of the sea, all must divide,'" Carina read. Her eyes grew wide. A tiny illustration of a landmass had also appeared beneath the constellation. "It's an island!" she exclaimed, unable to stop the smile spreading across her face. "The stars lead to an island!"

Carina laughed with relief. She finally had her clue! She was one step closer to finding her map, and the treasure—as long as Henry Turner kept up his end of the bargain.

With their combined effort, as well as a ship, they could sail to the island and find the Trident.

That is, Carina thought, *if I'm not hanged first.*

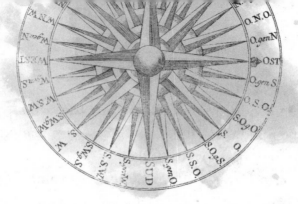

CHAPTER 24

MORNING ARRIVED, but Henry Turner did not. Carina awoke to a bright shaft of sunlight piercing the cell window—and the sound of heavy footsteps approaching down the prison hall.

"Good morning, witch," a soldier greeted her with a wicked smile. "Ready to die?"

Carina and several other accused individuals were led, shackled, to a cage on wheels. Once they were locked securely inside, the cage rumbled to the town square.

A large crowd had turned out again, this time to see the routine gallows executions.

Lieutenant Scarfield walked up to the cage, a smug sneer on his face. He looked Carina up and down. "Finally where you belong, I see?" he said. "Don't get too comfortable. I've personally seen to it that you're up first." He leaned in close. "I've been looking forward to this."

Carina's face was grim as the guards came to open the cage door and drag her up to the gallows. It wasn't looking good. She had placed all her hope in Henry Turner, but perhaps she had been mistaken.

I wonder if word of my death will make it back to England, she thought as the hangman adjusted a noose around her neck. Would any of them—Mrs. Altwood, Sarah or James, Lady Devonshire—ever know her fate?

Carina swallowed hard as she gazed out at the sea of jeering faces, cheering, laughing, enjoying the early-morning spectacle of death.

No, she realized with a sinking heart. *They will not.*

Across the square, a commotion caught her attention. The guards seemed to be having difficulty with another prisoner being led to the guillotine—a filthy man with long hair.

"Oh, you have got to be kidding me." Carina rolled her eyes.

"I'm not one to complain," Jack Sparrow said loudly as he was strapped down to the guillotine, "but this basket is full of heads. Could I get a fresh one?"

The hangman finished securing Carina's noose and stepped back. "Any last words, witch?" he said.

Carina breathed heavily and looked out again at the dimly lit eyes of the local revelers.

If she was going to die, she would do so in honor of her father—as a woman of science to the bitter end.

"The last words of Carina Smyth," she began. "Good sirs, I am not a witch. But I forgive your dim-wittedness and feeble brains. In short, most of you have the mind of a goat—"

"Is it not common practice for those being executed to be offered a last meal?" Jack cried out loudly from his guillotine, interrupting her.

"I believe I was making a point," Carina shouted in his direction. "If you could just be patient . . ."

"My head is about to be lopped off, hence the urgency," he retorted.

"And my neck is about to be broken," said Carina. *Unbelievable,* she thought. *That pirate sends me to my fate, and now he interrupts my final words!*

"On occasion, the neck doesn't break," Jack quipped.

Carina looked at him. "What?"

"I've seen men swing for hours," the pirate explained casually, "the life slowly choking out of them. Eyes bulging, tongue swelling, a revolting gurgling sound . . ."

"May I finish?" Carina snapped.

"The point is," Jack continued, "it's entirely possible you still have hours left to whisper your last words, whereas my head will soon be in this basket staring up at my lifeless body, which happens to be *famished*!"

Carina huffed. "Kill the filthy pirate. I'll wait."

"I wouldn't hear of it," Jack said. "Witches first."

"I am not a witch!" Carina exploded. "Were you not listening?"

"Hard to listen with the mind of a goat!" he yelled back.

"Enough!" shouted Lieutenant Scarfield. "Kill them both!"

The executioners stepped forward to throw the handles that would drop the guillotine blade and open Carina's trapdoor at the same time. That was it. The end had come.

And then, suddenly . . .

A heroic figure swooped down on a rope! Carina's eyes grew wide. It was Henry Turner! He was swinging down to help! The young man flew straight toward the executioner . . . and missed. Badly. He landed instead in the middle of the town square, tumbling in a cloud of dust while several soldiers quickly surrounded him. Henry struggled to fight them off as Lieutenant Scarfield stepped forward.

"Get another noose!" Scarfield ordered. "He will die with the others."

Scarfield walked up to Henry as the soldiers pinned his arms. "Did you think you could defeat us, boy?"

Henry smiled. "No, sir. I'm just the diversion. *Fire!*"

Instantly, an explosion rocked the town square. Carina watched in disbelief. What was happening? A band of pirates was dragging a cannon into the middle of the square.

Scarfield was furious. *"Pirates!"* he screamed.

The town square erupted into chaos. People and horses stampeded as the cannon exploded again, rocketing dirt and debris in every direction. Out of the corner of her eye, Carina caught a glimpse of Jack's guillotine just as it was hit by a cannonball. The entire platform began to spin. The blade whizzed down toward the pirate's neck only to be whipped up again in the nick of time before whizzing back down. This continued—with Jack escaping death by a hair-breadth each time—until, suddenly, a runaway cart smashed into the platform and the whole thing tipped. Men and women trampled past, and Carina gasped as Jack Sparrow disappeared from sight in a cloud of commotion. Surely he was done for.

Finally, the dust settled, and Carina couldn't believe her eyes. The pirate had been set free in the crash, the guillotine blade lying harmless at his feet.

"Gibbs!" Jack cried to one of the men fighting off the soldiers. "I knew you'd come crawling back!"

"The Turner boy paid us ten pieces of silver to save your neck," Gibbs replied.

Henry found a pirate crew to help! Carina realized.

At least, she hoped they would help her. She was still bound precariously by the noose. And if her platform shattered, it wouldn't be the rope that snapped, but her neck.

"Henry!" she heard Jack Sparrow call as he fought back three guards, using the guillotine blade as an impromptu weapon. "Find your witch!"

Carina couldn't believe that Henry knew such a nefarious

man. But now was not the time to think about such things. Carina struggled to free herself as a scruffy pirate battled a soldier directly in front of her. She watched helplessly as they drew closer and closer to her.

Then, to her surprise, the pirate bested the soldier, sending him off the gallows platform.

"Thank you," Carina said, relieved.

"M'lady." The pirate bowed, extending his arms out wide. Carina could see that one of his hands was headed straight for the gallows switch.

"No—" she started, but it was too late. The pirate hit the switch, and the floor dropped out from beneath her.

Carina screamed. Her neck would snap any second!

And then, miraculously, hands grabbed her.

Carina looked down and saw Henry standing below her, his arms round her lower half and his face buried in her navel as he used all his strength to hold her up.

Henry grinned. "From this moment on, we are to be allies," he said.

Relief washed over Carina. Henry had kept his promise—he had saved her.

Then she realized exactly where his hands were: holding her . . . *posterior.*

"Considering where your left hand is, I'd say we are more than that," Carina said.

An extremely embarrassed Henry tried to adjust his

position while making sure the rope around her neck did not grow taut. "We find the Trident together," Henry said, changing the subject. "Do I have your word?"

"You're holding everything *but* my word," Carina replied. "Now cut me down!"

"I don't have a sword at the moment," Henry said sheepishly.

Carina stared down at him. "You came to rescue me without a sword? What kind of soldier are you?"

Henry moved Carina out of the way of a nearby brawl between a pirate and a soldier. "Perhaps we could discuss this later, as I am having trouble hoisting your port!"

"You are far from port," Carina said, correcting him. "That is my stern!"

Henry looked up at her. "Are you sure?"

"Positive!"

"Well, look at this." Carina and Henry both turned toward the new voice.

Lieutenant Scarfield walked slowly toward them, sword drawn. "If I kill the coward, the witch hangs. Two for the price of one."

"Please do not let go!" Carina cried to Henry.

Henry watched, defenseless, as the huge soldier bore down on him. "Might be difficult when he kills me," he cried.

And then—

Whomp!

Scarfield flopped to the ground like a limp fish. Behind him stood Jack Sparrow. He'd knocked the soldier out cold with the blunt end of the guillotine blade.

Carina and Henry stared at Jack in disbelief. The pirate had saved them.

All around them, the commotion had died down. The soldiers had retreated, defeated by the pirate crew and their cannon. Now Jack and his men surrounded Henry and Carina.

To their surprise, the pirates all drew their swords.

"Gentlemen." Jack Sparrow smiled. "These two prisoners will lead us to the Trident."

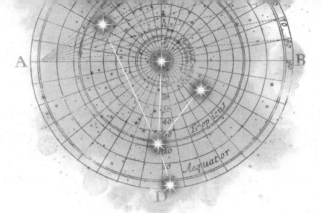

CHAPTER 25

CARINA SCOWLED AT HENRY as they stood side by side, tied to the mast of the pirate's ship, the *Dying Gull*.

"So this was your brilliant plan?" she asked. "To be tortured and killed by pirates?"

"That is Captain Jack Sparrow," Henry explained, nodding in the filthy pirate's direction. "One of the greatest pirates to ever sail the Caribbean. And we have an accord—he and his crew will sail with us to find the Trident."

Carina looked down at the ropes binding them. "Will that be before or after they have us walk the plank?"

"We needed a ship!" Henry said, defending himself.

"You call this a ship?" Carina asked.

As far as ships went, the *Dying Gull* was, well, dying. To

Carina's eye it appeared little more than a piecemeal raft with a lopsided mast and so many holes it was a wonder they hadn't sunk. Just getting it in the water had been a challenge for Sparrow's crew. The first mate's cry of "Prepare to drown!" had not been reassuring.

All the while, Jack had continually groaned that his true ship, the *Black Pearl*, was trapped in a glass bottle. Carina could only assume it was the rum talking.

"These men are mad," she said pointedly to Henry.

"These men are pirates," Henry said. "They know what they're doing." Then his face grew dark. "Carina, there's something you need to know. The dead are sailing straight for us."

Carina scoffed. The pirates might not be the only mad ones on this "ship." She wanted to trust Henry. Truly, she did. But the way he talked of ghosts and curses as though they were real greatly irritated her.

"Is that so?" she asked.

"Yes," Henry insisted. "I've spoken with them. A sea captain named Salazar has returned from the dead to hunt Jack Sparrow. His ghost ship, the *Silent Mary*, and crew attacked the ship I was serving on and left me alone alive to tell the tale. Salazar is death itself. He will not rest until he has destroyed Jack and all pirates along with him."

There was a brief pause as Henry's words sunk in. "Have you spoken to krakens and mermaids as well?" Carina asked ironically.

"Krakens don't speak—everyone knows that," Henry said.

That about did it. Carina had risked her neck to free Henry and had wound up in a noose and tied to the mast of a pirate ship because of it. And worse, the degenerate captain had taken Galileo's diary while his men tied her up. "I never should have saved you!" Carina exclaimed.

Henry paused, clearly realizing that Carina wasn't going to believe him. He seemed to choose his next words carefully. "Last night, there was a blood moon," he said, "just as you described. Tell me what it revealed."

"And why should I trust you?" Carina snapped.

"Tell me what you found," Henry pleaded, trying to get her back on his side, "and I promise to help you."

Carina turned away. "I've been alone my entire life. I don't need any help." She realized the truth of those words as she said them. All her past allies had left her life in one way or another, and none of them had ever really understood the dreams she'd had for her future. She'd learned that she could rely only on herself to make them happen.

"Then why did you come to me, Carina?" Henry asked, pressing her. "Why are we tied together in the middle of the sea, chasing the same treasure? Maybe you don't see it, but our destiny is undeniable."

Carina pulled a face. "I don't believe in destiny," she muttered.

"Then believe in me," Henry said, "as I believe in you."

Carina sighed. He was looking at her so earnestly, with

so much hope and conviction. Deep down, she *wanted* to believe in Henry, to believe in all this: that somehow, fate had led her on the right course toward discovering her birthright and honoring her father. But everything in the past few days had happened so quickly and, worse, was out of her control. She hated that feeling. She wanted to be on course again—in line with the stars.

"The moon revealed a clue," Carina admitted. "'To release the power of the sea, all must divide.'" She told him about the illustration of the island.

"Divide?" asked Henry. "What does it mean?"

"I don't know," Carina said. It didn't make sense. And she was now starting to second-guess everything.

Henry offered her a reassuring look. "Then we'll just have to find out."

Just then, Jack Sparrow sauntered up, brandishing Galileo's diary.

"There is no map in this map," he said.

"Give me that diary!" Carina exclaimed.

"Give me the Map No Man Can Read," said Jack.

"If you could read it, then it wouldn't be called the Map No *Man* Can Read," Carina replied.

"I beg you not to argue with her," Henry said with a sigh.

"Most of the men on this ship can't read," Jack told Carina. "That makes all maps the Map No Man Can Read."

Carina huffed. "If no one can read it, then you have no use for it or me."

Jack frowned. "Let me start again. Show me the map!"

"I can't, as it does not yet exist!" Carina exclaimed.

A pirate named Marty leaned over to one of the other crewmen on deck. "She's a witch," he whispered.

"No, I'm an astronomer," Carina said, correcting him, sick and tired of the witch nonsense.

"So . . . you breed donkeys?" another pirate, named Scrum, asked.

"What?" Carina asked. "No—an astronomer contemplates the sky."

"On a donkey?" asked Scrum.

"There is no donkey!" Carina shouted.

"Then how do you breed them?" a third pirate asked.

Carina felt like her head was about to explode.

"She's a witch!" exclaimed Marty. "We should throw her overboard!"

The pirates all stepped forward; none of them wanted dark magic sailing aboard their vessel.

Jack moved between them and Carina. "Allow me to simplify the equation," he said, pacifying his men. Jack turned to Carina. "Give me the map, or I'll kill him."

Jack drew a pistol and aimed it at Henry. Carina's stomach lurched inexplicably, but she kept her face calm.

"Go ahead and kill him," Carina said, challenging him. "You're bluffing."

"And you're blushing." Jack smirked. "Throw him over!"

Abruptly, the pirates untied Henry and Carina from the

mast and rebound Henry's hands. They shoved him toward the rail of the ship.

"He doesn't appear to be bluffing!" Henry called to Carina.

"We call this keelhauling," Jack explained. "Young Henry will be tossed over and dragged under the ship."

Carina made sure to appear unfazed. "Go on. What are you waiting for?"

Henry shot Carina a look before the pirates gagged him—and tossed him over the edge of the ship.

Carina used all her willpower to act like she didn't care. These filthy pirates wouldn't really kill Henry, not after he'd helped them rescue their captain from the chopping block.

Would they?

"Not a very strong swimmer," Jack noted casually, peering over.

"Just went under the ship!" Gibbs observed. "If he's lucky, he'll drown before the barnacles slice him to bits."

"Barnacles?" Carina asked, feeling dread starting to creep in.

Jack walked to her and leaned close by her face. "Like a thousand knives across your back," he said. "And of course, the blood attracts sharks."

"Sharks?" asked Carina. Henry had been overboard for several minutes now. Why weren't they hauling him up?

"Shark off the bow!" Gibbs suddenly called.

Jack shrugged. "I'd say swimming is no longer his primary concern."

Carina couldn't help it: she was growing very worried. "We're wasting time," she snapped. "Bring him up!"

"All of him?" Jack raised an eyebrow. "Because that might be a problem in a few minutes."

"The map is there!" Carina cried, pointing hastily straight up toward the sky.

Everyone paused, looking at her.

"On your finger?" Marty asked.

"It's in the heavens!" shouted Carina. "That diary will lead me to a map hidden in the stars."

Jack pondered that. "A treasure map hidden in the stars?"

"Someone must have an enormous quill," Scrum added.

"Bring him up, and I will find it tonight!" Carina exclaimed.

Jack smiled. "Sorry, can't bring him up. Look for yourself."

Carina rushed to the rail and looked over. She couldn't believe her eyes. There was Henry, safe and sound. He hadn't been in the water at all. The pirates had dropped him to a rowboat tied to the side of the ship. Henry looked up at her, gag still stuffed in his mouth, hands bound behind his back.

Without meaning to, Carina sighed in relief.

Jack walked up to her side. "As I said . . . blushing."

CHAPTER 26

LATER THAT NIGHT, Carina stood at the bow of the ship, watching the sky. Waiting.

Out of the corner of her eye, she caught a glimpse of Henry, also staring out over the sea. He looked pensive. Troubled. In a way that Carina could tell was very real.

She walked over to him.

"What are you doing?" she asked.

"Looking for him," Henry answered. "Even when I know he's not there. My father."

Carina studied Henry's face. She had known him for only a few days. And yet there was no denying their paths were very similar. Carina hadn't met many young men in her life. James and the other boys at the orphanage had just been childhood friends, and there had never been time or opportunity for socializing at Hanover Hall. But Carina felt drawn to Henry. It was as though Carina had finally found the right person to talk to about the things that mattered most to her.

"Just because you can't see something doesn't mean it's not there," she told him, using his own words of encouragement.

Henry turned to her. "Like the map?"

He does understand. Carina smiled. *He knows how important it is.*

"I have to find it," Carina said.

"No one has ever found it," Henry replied.

Carina reached to take Henry's hand. She was just about to say, "Together, we will," when Henry finished his thought. "Maybe it doesn't exist," he said quietly.

Carina gasped, taken aback. "What did you say?"

Henry realized his mistake. "Nothing," he lied.

But Carina could feel her temper bubbling. *Why does he keep doing this? Every time we have a nice moment, he ruins it by saying something foolish about legends or ghosts. And now he questions the map?*

"Doesn't exist?" she asked angrily. She held up the diary and walked toward Henry, forcing him back against the rail. "This diary is the only truth I know. I kept it with me every day in that orphanage, studied the heavens when it was forbidden—when they called me a witch! I swore to know the sky as my father intended me to."

"Your father?" Henry asked, surprised.

"My mother died as I was born," Carina explained. "This diary was all that was left with me—"

"I know what it is to grow up without a father, Carina," Henry said, interrupting her.

"Then you know I can never stop," she said heatedly.

To her surprise, Henry reached out to grasp her hands, sending an inexplicable electric charge through her. "Carina, you're always looking to the sky. Perhaps the answer is right here."

Carina flushed. What did he mean by that?

Then she noticed his hands were not on hers, but on the diary.

"Show me," Henry said.

Carina took a deep breath and opened the book to the page with Galileo's most important passage: *Tutte le verità saranno comprese quando le stesse si saranno derectus.*

"Galileo wrote that 'all truths will be understood once the stars align,'" Carina said.

Henry furrowed his brow. "If the stars do not move, how can they align?"

"He could be referring to the planets," Carina suggested.

"But he clearly drew stars." Henry pointed to the cluster of five stars in the drawing.

"He wrote the word *derectus*," Carina said. "So the stars must align."

Henry looked at the diary, then at Carina.

"Galileo was Italian. But *derectus* is *not* Italian. It's Latin."

Carina paused. "Latin?" she asked, uncertain. She'd never thought of the diary being in anything but Italian. And for all his ravings about the supernatural, Henry did seem impressively learned.

"*Derectus* does not mean 'align,'" Henry continued. "It means 'a straight line.'"

Carina considered that. "All truths will be understood once the stars are in a straight line," she said slowly.

Suddenly, her eyes grew wide.

"What is it?" Henry asked.

"It was right in front of me!" Carina exclaimed, hardly daring to believe that this might, at long last, be the final clue. "There is a straight line moving from Orion—the son of Poseidon!"

"But how do you follow it?" Henry asked, confused.

"It starts with the ruby." Carina's heart thumped. "A straight line from the ruby . . ."

She took the ruby from the front cover and held it to the sky like a lens. Carefully, she looked through it, positioning the gem over the constellation Orion. Henry moved beside her so he might look as well.

And then she saw it! A burning red line running straight across the sky.

"Do you see that?" Henry gasped.

Before their eyes, red lines visible only through the ruby lens charted a course across the heavens . . . a map!

"A straight line starting in Orion," Carina said excitedly. "The hunter's arrow moving straight through Cassiopeia . . . heading across the sky toward the end of the Southern Cross! It ends there, Henry!"

Carina pointed to the Southern Cross, blazing in the sky through the ruby.

"So the map is inside the cross?" Henry asked.

"No, because it's not a cross, it's an X!" Carina cried. "The Southern Cross is an X hidden in the sky since the beginning of time!"

Carina looked at Henry, her eyes shining.

"This is the Map No Man Can Read!"

Henry grinned. "That map will lead us to the Trident. We just have to follow the X!"

Suddenly, the sound of guns cocking broke their elation.

Jack was standing behind them, along with his crew— a familiar scene. Except this time they were all pointing pistols.

"And X always marks the spot," Jack said.

CHAPTER 27

IMMEDIATELY, JACK ORDERED Carina to guide them to the X in the sky. Carina wasn't keen on taking orders from pirates—at gunpoint. But seeing as how she needed a ship to reach the Southern Cross anyway, she didn't have much choice but to work with them.

The rest of that night, Jack, Gibbs, Scrum, and the rest of the crew watched as Carina studied the sky, a ticking chronometer in her hand.

She continued to gaze upward well past sunrise, never saying a word. By midday, the pirates were extremely confused.

"So she's saying she has the map, but only she can follow it?" Gibbs asked the others.

A pirate named Bollard frowned. "So . . . we should shoot her?" he suggested.

"Leave her be," Henry said, annoyed. "She's finding it."

"You've been saying that for hours," another man, named Cremble, said accusingly.

"There are two things I know to be true," Scrum whispered to Jack. "Stars do not shine by day, and she did not bring her donkey."

A crewman named Pike piped up. "Do any of you see this X?"

Scrum shielded his eyes from the sun. "I see a bird . . . a cloud . . . my own hand . . ."

Gibbs sighed, exasperated. "Jack, how are we to follow an X to a spot where no land could exist? An X which has disappeared with the sun?"

"This may very well be the worst map I've ever seen," Jack admitted. "Mainly because I can't see it." Without warning, Jack grabbed Carina. "For the last time, how do we find your X?"

"This chronometer keeps the exact time in London," Carina snapped. "I'm making an altitude measurement to the Southern Cross to determine longitude. Only then will we find that spot on the sea."

The pirates all looked at one another.

"Witch!" cried Marty.

"You expect to follow your X with a timepiece?" Gibbs asked, even more confused.

Carina nodded. "My calculations are precise and true. I'm not just an astronomer. I'm also a horologist."

To Carina's surprise, the pirates all stared at her sympathetically.

"No shame in that, dear," Jack finally said. "We all have to earn a living."

"No, I'm a *horologist*," Carina repeated.

"So was my mum," Scrum admitted. "Although she didn't crow about it quite as loud as you."

"*Horology* is the study of time!" Carina exclaimed.

Jack frowned. "So nobody can find that X but you?" he asked.

"And the donkey?" Scrum added.

Carina was about to retort when Henry suddenly cried out behind her.

"Salazar!"

Everyone spun to see an enormous vessel bearing down on them a few miles back.

"Ship to the aft!" Gibbs cried.

The terrified crew all wheeled on Jack.

"The dead were not part of this deal!" Gibbs exclaimed.

"We should never have followed a luckless pirate and a witch to sea!" cried Pike.

"Our own captain is leading us to slaughter!" shouted Cremble.

Carina watched in disbelief as the pirate crew drew their swords and surrounded her, Henry, and Jack. Did those fools actually believe they were being chased by the dead? She wouldn't have thought it possible if she hadn't been able to see the dread clear in their eyes.

"We've been fooled for the last time," rasped Scrum.

"Kill them all!" another cried.

Carina and Henry drew close together. But Jack raised his hands to stop them.

"Kill me, and the dead won't have their revenge!" Jack pointed out.

"Which will anger them even more," Henry added.

Carina looked from the pirates to Jack to Henry. "Are all pirates this stupid?" she whispered.

Meanwhile, the crew was now terrified *and* confused. The dead would kill them all if they caught up to the *Dying Gull*. But if the crew killed Jack, then the dead would *still* kill them all as revenge for killing the man they were hunting.

"Jack, what should we do?" Gibbs asked desperately.

Jack shrugged. "As captain, might I suggest a mutiny?"

* * *

Jack, Carina, and Henry sat aboard a longboat, adrift at sea. The *Dying Gull* grew smaller and smaller on the horizon.

"Mutiny?" Carina asked with annoyance. "You had to suggest a munity?"

"Carina, they're coming," Henry warned, rowing feverishly with Jack.

"Ghosts?" Carina asked, tired of the word. "You're both afraid of ghosts?"

"Yes," said Jack. "And lizards and Quakers."

"Well, I choose not to believe." Carina crossed her arms.

"Do you not see what's behind us?" Henry insisted.

Sighing, Carina turned in the boat and looked behind them. Not more than a mile back, Salazar's ship, the *Silent Mary*, was gaining on them. Carina shielded her eyes. It was a ship at sea—nothing out of the ordinary about that. Though now that she could see it more closely, it did look odd. Ominous. The sails were torn, but it was sailing at an unholy speed. That was strange. And was the hull . . . rotted through? It seemed almost to resemble a large floating rib cage. Dark clouds gathered behind the ship, although the rest of the sky remained clear.

Carina shook her head and shrugged. She couldn't believe Henry's ravings had started to get to her for a moment. "I see a very old ship," she said to Henry. "Nothing more."

Suddenly, several more enormous sails unfurled from the *Silent Mary*'s mast. The ship picked up even more speed.

Carina frowned. Now that *was* concerning. Regardless of who was aboard that ship, it was clear they were after them—more specifically, Jack.

Carina looked ahead. She saw a small island not far from them.

There was only one choice.

She stood abruptly and began to unbutton her dress.

"What are you doing?" Henry asked in alarm.

"Preparing to swim," Carina said matter-of-factly. "Whoever those men are, they're after Jack. And Jack is on this boat. So I am going to swim for it."

Jack pulled a face, offended. "How dare you do exactly what I would do if I were you."

Without further argument, Carina stripped off her dress so that she was down to her undergarments, which covered most of her body anyway. Then she dove into the bracing water.

"Carina!" Henry cried as she swam hard and fast toward the shore. But she didn't turn.

She just swam and swam. The ocean current fought strongly against her. It felt as though the closer she got to shore, the rougher the waves became. Odd—had someone called "Shark!" behind her?

Still, Carina didn't turn. Instead, she focused all her energy on reaching the shore. Her arms and lungs burned with effort. The island was so close she was certain she would feel the sandbar under her at any moment. She could be no more than twenty feet away . . . ten feet away . . .

And then success! The water became shallow and Carina's feet hit land. Gasping, she stumbled ashore, exhausted and out of breath. She collapsed to the sand. She had made it.

FWOOM!

Jack and Henry suddenly crashed up alongside her in the longboat, sending sand flying in her face.

"What is wrong with you both?" Carina exclaimed angrily.

But Henry didn't even look at her; he just continued staring out to sea, his expression consumed with fear.

"Carina, don't turn around," he warned.

"Let me guess," Carina said sarcastically. "You've seen another—"

As she spoke, Carina finally turned around.

And she froze in terror.

Chapter 28

WHAT SHE WAS SEEING WASN'T POSSIBLE . . . wasn't conceivable. . . .

Standing on the sea was an entire army of the dead.

The *dead*!

"Ah—ah—" Carina tried to speak, but her voice was reduced to a squeak.

There was no denying it: the grotesque souls leering at them were definitely *not* members of the living. Some had deep gashes sliced across their chests: angry, ripped wounds rotting from the inside out. Others were missing their chests altogether, leaving gaping holes through which

Carina could see tempestuous clouds opening up in the skies behind them.

Their clothes were decrepit; their limbs hung at odd angles. And in front of this ghastly crew from beyond the grave stood a captain—proud, tall, and cruel—with half his skull gruesomely blasted off in the back.

"Jack Sparrow," rasped Captain Salazar through black teeth. He sneered and brandished a rotting sword.

Carina clutched her mouth in horror as several ghosts rushed forward, reaching hungrily for Jack. But as soon as their tortured souls hit the border of the shore, they snapped back violently as though shocked. With horrible shrieks, their spirits disintegrated, seeming to die a second death.

"They can't step on land!" Jack cried in relief. "And to think I was worried."

Carina recoiled. Her voice finally returned, and she screamed a single word. . . .

"Ghosts!"

"Do you remember me, Jack?" Captain Salazar said in a low, fierce voice.

Jack conceded. "You look the same. Other than that gaping hole in your skull. Are those new boots?"

"You'll soon pay the devil his due!" Salazar cried.

Carina had had enough. She ran.

"Ghosts!" she screamed again, taking off into the island jungle.

"Carina!" Henry cried behind her. "Stop!"

But Carina did not stop—she couldn't stop. She could do only one thing at the moment, and that was *run*. Run as far away as possible from that horrific, dreadful, *impossible* scene at the shore.

It's not possible! she told herself over and over again, crashing through grasses and ducking under palm branches. *Not possible, not possible, not possible!*

It was like a hole had been torn in the fabric of her reality, forcing her to get a glimpse of hell she never should have witnessed. Her entire life had been governed by the rational. All those years she'd clung to the truth. And now . . . *how* could she possibly rationalize this away?

She couldn't. That was why she needed to get away. As far away as—

THWAP!

"Ahhhhh!" Carina screamed.

She swooped up toward the sky, her arms and legs tangled in a mesh of rope. Carina's heart pounded so hard she could barely see.

A net—she'd been caught in a hunter's net.

The grasses and palm branches and tree roots all swam dizzyingly far below her. She dangled precariously high above the ground, completely helpless.

Unable to take any more, Carina blacked out.

* * *

When Carina's vision returned, she didn't remember what had happened. She seemed to be caught in a net, swaying some thirty feet off the ground.

Suddenly, the events from the beach flooded back. An army of the dead—bloodthirsty and looking to kill—had been standing on the sea.

She started to make the net rock, though all it seemed to do was nauseate her. The rope was thick and sturdy, not a lock she could pick. An ocean of dread came over her. She couldn't escape alone. As much as she loathed the fact, she needed . . .

"Help!" she screamed desperately over and over again. *"Help me!"*

Just as Carina's voice grew hoarse, footsteps crashed through the jungle. She watched anxiously as two figures approached.

Henry and Jack.

"Carina!" Henry exclaimed. He moved to scale the tree, but suddenly, both he *and* Jack were swooped up in trappers' nets, too.

"No!" Carina exclaimed, her heart sinking.

Now all three of them swung helplessly from a clump of trees.

"Some rescue," Carina muttered under her breath. "Now what do we do?"

It seemed it would be up to her to figure out a plan. Carina was just considering rocking herself toward Henry so that they might weaken the branches holding them, when she suddenly saw a strange man standing near the trees' roots. Carina stared, wide-eyed. She hadn't noticed him before. He must have arrived when she'd blacked out. He was grizzled and filthy and carried a gun.

The man smiled knowingly as he approached Jack, who hung lower in his net than Carina and Henry did in theirs. Then he clocked the pirate with the butt of his gun, knocking him out cold.

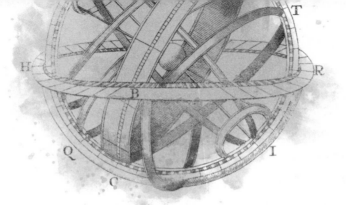

CHAPTER 29

CARINA, HENRY, and the unconscious Jack were dragged to the edge of the jungle, where a dilapidated village was set up. Carina noticed with disgust that the locals had constructed a makeshift chapel out of the giant skeleton of a beached whale. Rickety chairs were set up beneath the rib cage like pews, and at the front, beneath the gaping bony mouth of the once monstrous creature, stood a jagged stone altar.

The men shoved Henry and Jack into the chapel while the women forced Carina to don a tattered red gown. They pulled at her hair, arranging dead flowers among her curls.

"Henry, what is happening?" Carina called.

Henry shook his head. "I wish I knew."

Carina looked around at the bizarre scene. The villagers were dressed in what they must have considered finery, but it was all twisted and wrong. The women's gowns were colorful yet torn and filthy. The men's hats bore exotic feathers bent and askew. It was more like a vision from a freakish nightmare than a church congregation.

From soldiers and mutinies to the supernatural and now . . . this. Carina grimaced. *How far off course must I travel at the hands of Jack Sparrow?*

Carina's thoughts were interrupted by villagers pressing guns against her and Henry's backs. They shoved them inside the chapel while Jack was dropped unceremoniously in front of the altar.

The man who had knocked Jack out directed a crowd of twenty or so unsightly miscreants to seats. Then a round woman holding a bouquet of dead flowers began to walk down the aisle. As she moved closer, Carina could see her face was terribly scarred, and scabbed sores lined her mouth. The woman smiled, exposing rotten yellow teeth.

That was when Jack woke up.

"Time to pay your debt, Sparrow," the man with the gun sneered.

Jack looked up in surprise. "Pig Kelly, my old friend!" he exclaimed.

Pig Kelly raised his gun to Jack's head. "'Friend'? You

hear that, boys? This lying pirate owes me a plunder of silver! But luck has brought him to Hangman's Bay—and he'll settle his debt here and now."

"Of course, Pig, I've looked everywhere for you," Jack said, trying to explain himself. "I prayed for your safety after inadvertently paying those men to put you in a sack. Name your price."

"Her *name* is Beatrice," Pig Kelly said. "And she's my poor widowed sister."

Jack grimaced as the woman with the dead flowers stepped up close beside him. She eyed him hungrily, as though he were a piece of meat.

"Let's get on with it," she rasped.

"She's a midwife," Pig Kelly explained. "Been looking for a respectable man, but they don't come to this horrid place. So you'll do."

"I'll do what?" Jack asked, unnerved.

"Make an honest woman of her." Pig Kelly laughed. "This is how you'll clear your debt. Congratulations, Jack. It's your wedding day!"

Jack recoiled in disgust as Beatrice pulled a torn veil over her face.

"We'll honeymoon in the barn," she whispered.

With a scream, Jack tried to run, but Pig Kelly's men had tied a noose around his neck, attaching him to the altar. He was trapped.

"Let us begin," a terrified priest squeaked from the altar.

"Bring the best man and bridesmaid!" cried Pig Kelly.

Several men shoved Henry and Carina closer toward the altar.

"Let me go!" Carina exclaimed.

That made the men laugh.

"Pretty girl, Jack," said Pig Kelly. "No wonder you were chasing after her. She'll die by your side if you fail to say 'I do.'"

"Place your hand on the Bible," the priest instructed.

"I have scabies . . ." Jack warned Beatrice.

Beatrice laid her head on his shoulder. "So do I."

"Say 'I do,'" Pig Kelly repeated, "or I'll put a bullet in your skull."

Jack glanced sideways at Beatrice.

"Promise me you won't miss?" he asked.

"They're about to kill us!" Henry shouted at Jack.

"Say 'I do'!" Carina urged him.

"I'm trying." Jack swallowed hard. "Having a bit of a mid-wife crisis."

Pig Kelly and his men all cocked their guns.

"Last chance," Pig Kelly said menacingly.

Carina looked at Henry pleadingly. "Do something!" she whispered.

Suddenly, a look crossed Henry's face. "Wait!" he exclaimed. "This is not legal."

Catching on, Carina joined in. "He's right! Does any man here object to these nuptials?"

"I do!" cried Jack.

"Congratulations!" the priest declared, misinterpreting Jack's words. "You may now kiss the—"

Bang! Bang! Bang!

Loud gun blasts suddenly rang out. For a moment, Carina thought they had been fired upon. But then she saw the whale skeleton splintering above them. The blasts had been aimed at the chapel.

Everyone turned. A man holding a smoking blunderbuss stood at the entrance to the chapel—along with a pirate crew.

"Hector Barbossa!" exclaimed Jack. "Who invited you to my wedding?"

Carina studied the sea captain standing at the opening of the whale skeleton. Hector Barbossa was a gnarled, weathered man, dressed in a rich naval coat trimmed in gold. Though he was aged, his eyes were sharp. Long curled hair spilled out from under his three-cornered captain's hat. Carina imagined the captain had seen many a battle at sea.

"I always knew you'd settle down eventually," Barbossa said to Jack, his voice gravelly.

"Did you bring me a present?" Jack asked hopefully.

Bang! Bang! Without warning, Barbossa shot Pig Kelly in the leg.

All the locals screamed. Chaos erupted as everyone

scattered. Several men picked up Pig Kelly and hauled him away while a tearful Beatrice followed, dead flowers trailing behind her.

"Old Kelly has seen worse," she heard one of the locals mutter.

"Thanks, Hector," Jack said, breathing a sigh of relief. "It's just what I've always wanted." He looked Barbossa up and down. "I must say, you look marvelous."

"And I'm amazed you've maintained your youthful appearance," Barbossa said, returning the compliment.

"I've missed you so much," said Jack.

"I know!" exclaimed Barbossa.

"Do you know who this man is?" Carina whispered to Henry.

Henry shrugged. "Never seen him before in my life."

Carina noticed Barbossa's pirate crew shifting uncomfortably.

"Um, Captain Barbossa," one of the men said, "shouldn't we be getting back to Salazar so we can trade Jack's life for our own?"

Henry and Carina stiffened. So the men were in league with Salazar!

"Aye, we could do that." Barbossa nodded slowly. "But I have come for the Trident of Poseidon!"

Barbossa's men murmured in alarm.

"You're going to double-cross the dead?" one of them asked.

"And with the Trident," Barbossa continued, "I will *gut* the dead who stole my command of the sea!"

Jack raised a hand to protest. "As much as I love this plan, there are two small problems. Firstly, I don't wish to die. Secondly, no vessel can outrun that shipwreck."

"But there is one, Jack." Barbossa tapped Jack's coat with the tip of his sword. A faint *tink* of glass echoed beneath the lapel.

"And she be the fastest ship at sea," Barbossa said. "The *Pearl*. Entrapped in that bottle by Blackbeard five winters ago."

Unexpectedly, Barbossa began waving his sword in a ritualistic circle above his head. "By the power of that blackguard's sovereign blade, I hereby release the *Black Pearl* to claim her former glory!"

The pirate captain stabbed his sword—straight toward Jack's heart.

Carina gasped. She couldn't believe it; surely it was a mortal blow.

But Jack appeared unharmed.

The distinct sound of glass vibrating came from under Jack's coat. Water—not blood—oozed through the fabric, and something rumbled beneath the lapel.

"Ooh, Hector," Jack said. "I think my waters have broken."

Moments later, they were all back at the beach.

"It's coming!" Jack cried as the miniature ship in a bottle strapped to his side began to grow. Carina recalled Jack's ravings on the *Dying Gull* about the tiny ship in the bottle being his true vessel. But that had all just been drunken ravings. Hadn't it?

"She needs the sea!" Barbossa cried, quickly grabbing the ship from Jack and flinging it into the water.

Everyone watched in amazement as the water where Barbossa had tossed the ship bubbled and boiled. *FWOOM!* The full-sized *Black Pearl* exploded from beneath the surface. The ship stood, tall and majestic—a vision of glory upon the waves.

Carina couldn't believe her eyes. It just wasn't possible. But then again, neither were ghosts. "I don't believe it," she whispered. "A ship grown from . . . from . . ."

"Magic!" exclaimed Henry, his eyes twinkling.

Jack smiled brilliantly at his restored ship. It looked like his luck was finally turning around.

Then a gun was cocked at his head.

"There be room for only one captain, Jack," Barbossa said, chuckling. "Time to race the dead."

Chapter 30

THE *BLACK PEARL* CHARGED through the ocean, cutting its way across the water. Though it defied all logic and conflicted with every law of physics Carina had studied, somehow the ship had been restored, released from a bottle and grown to full size.

And time to reach the treasure was running out.

Swiftly, Barbossa and his men tied Jack to the center mast while Henry and Carina were lashed to the back mast near the helm. For what seemed like the hundredth time that week, Carina had been taken prisoner, bound against her will, and carried off course from her mission.

She was *not* happy.

Carina stared hard at Captain Barbossa, who was minding the wheel. The man was clearly relishing his return to glory, a devilish monkey sitting atop his shoulder. He offered the only hope of reaching the treasure. For now, it seemed, she had to play along.

"The course you sail must be exact, Captain," she called in a strong voice.

"There is no *exact* at sea," Barbossa replied without looking back.

"You need to listen to her, Captain," Henry urged him. "She's the only one who can follow the X."

That got Barbossa's attention. He strode over to Henry and Carina and leaned in close.

"Is that a fact?" he hissed in Henry's face. "This girl knows more of the sea than I?"

"You'll follow the Southern Cross to a single reflection point," Carina said, forging on. "I have a chronometer which determines longitude—which will take us to an exact spot at sea."

"Captain, you don't have to understand her," Henry insisted. "Just believe her."

Barbossa pondered that for a moment. He looked at the stars, and then at his men.

"Untie them," he ordered his crew.

"Sir?" one of his men asked, confused.

"Untie them!" Barbossa commanded.

Jumping to attention, Barbossa's crew released Henry and Carina from their restraints.

Barbossa stared at Carina for a long moment. "Take the wheel, miss," he finally said.

Barbossa's men sucked in their breath.

"Sir, you wouldn't allow a woman to steer your ship . . . ?" one of them asked, alarmed.

But Barbossa looked back at the *Silent Mary*, pursuing them far in the distance. "She'll follow her star or we'll all die together," he determined.

The crew watched in shock as Carina stepped up toward the wheel.

Carina glared at them. "What are you looking at?" she demanded. "Full to starboard, you indolent scalawags!"

* * *

Later that night, Carina stood at the helm of the *Black Pearl*, steering the ship.

It was quiet. Most of the crew had gone belowdecks. Carina breathed in the sea air deeply. She was on her way to completing the quest she had been on her whole life, to solving the puzzle that had consumed her every waking hour. By all accounts, she should've been excited. But so much had happened, and there hadn't been time before to think about everything. To let it sink in.

She gazed around the *Black Pearl*, trying to make sense of it all.

Henry moved up beside her.

"This ship—those ghosts," Carina began. "There can be no logical explanation."

"The myths of the sea are real, Carina," Henry said softly. "As real as my father."

Carina looked deep into Henry's brown eyes. They shone under the starlight, and he seemed to be looking at her as if she were the only other person in the world. Carina wondered what he was thinking. And then he spoke again.

"I'm glad you can see you were wrong."

Carina blinked. *Oh, no you don't,* she thought, shaking her head.

"Wrong?" she asked. "Perhaps I had some doubts. Thought you were mad. One could say I was possibly, arguably a bit . . ."

"Wrong," Henry said. "The word is *wrong!*"

Carina fought a smile. He looked rather earnest and sweet. And she supposed there *had* been something to the ridiculous stories he had been telling. She recalled how frustrating it had been when Lady Devonshire had thought her goal of finding the Trident was a fool's errand. Still, she enjoyed teasing him a bit. "Slightly in error," she replied.

Henry ran his fingers through his hair, a gesture Carina had grown to like. "This is the worst apology I've ever heard."

"Apology?" Carina asked with mock indignation. "Why would I apologize?"

"Because we've been chased by the dead," Henry said, leaning in close. "We sail on a ship raised from a bottle. Where is your science in that?"

"It was science which found that map," Carina pointed out.

"No, *we* found it. Together!" Henry insisted.

"Fine," Carina said, sighing. "Then I will apologize."

"Go on, then," said Henry.

Carina shrugged, a mischievous glint in her eye. "If I'm wrong, I'm wrong."

"Then say it."

Carina snorted. "One could argue that you owe *me* an apology, as my life has been threatened by pirates and dead men."

"Which you now believe in, I'm sorry to say," Henry said.

Carina nodded, her eyes twinkling. "Apology accepted."

Henry groaned in exasperation, though Carina noticed that the edge of his mouth twitched in amusement. "I'm going to the lookout."

Carina, now grinning widely, watched him go. "I'm glad you see it my way!"

CHAPTER 31

THE WATERS GREW ROUGH as the *Black Pearl* continued on its course. Wind howled, blowing Carina's hair back from her face. But she kept the wheel true. All the while, the *Silent Mary* pursued them relentlessly yet never gained ground.

Captain Barbossa moved up beside Carina, taking note of her course. Suddenly, a glint at her side caught his attention.

"Where did you get this, missy?" he asked, pointing to Galileo's diary. "I know this book."

"I would doubt you have read Galileo's diary," Carina replied snippily.

"This book be pirate treasure," Barbossa said, "stolen from an Italian ship many years ago."

"Stolen?" Carina felt her old temper flare. "You're mistaken."

"There was a ruby on the cover I'd not soon forget," Barbossa replied.

Haughtily, Carina produced the ruby from her dress pocket. "This was given to me by my father, who was clearly a man of science."

Barbossa's monkey scrambled up and snatched the ruby away from her. It handed the gemstone to the captain, chattering wildly.

"He was clearly a common thief," Barbossa said.

Carina could not hold herself back any longer. She slapped Barbossa across the face—hard. How *dare* he insult her father like that!

"The memory of my father will not be defiled by the tongue of a pirate!" she exclaimed. "This diary is my birthright, left with me on the steps of a children's home along with a name. Nothing more."

Carina's cheeks burned with anger. She expected Barbossa to retaliate.

But to her surprise, the captain paled. He stepped back, an odd expression crossing his face.

"Oh, so you're an orphan?" he asked. "And what be you called?"

"The brightest star in the north gave me my name," Carina replied proudly.

Barbossa's eyes narrowed, and the wrinkles crossing his

face seemed to deepen. "That would be Carina," he said somberly.

Carina looked up, the captain's reply startling her. "Carina Smyth," she said. "So you do know the stars?"

"I'm a captain," Barbossa answered. "I know which stars to follow home."

Carina watched as Barbossa stepped away. He headed over to Jack, who was still tied to the mast. The two men spoke quietly.

Odd, Carina thought. *No one has ever recognized my name as being that of a star. Even Lady Devonshire needed a moment to place it. How strange that the first person to realize it would be a pirate.*

Just then, Henry ran down from the lookout. "Redcoats!" he cried, sounding the alarm.

Barbossa left Jack and hurried to the ship rail.

Everyone clambered up to the deck to see a vessel sailing toward them—the British warship *Essex*.

"She's coming in starboard!" yelled Barbossa. "We'll fight to the last. The *Pearl* will not be taken from me again!"

Giant waves blasted the side of the *Pearl* as the warship approached. Carina struggled to keep the wheel, but it was slipping from her grasp. Henry raced up alongside her to help.

Through the blustering ocean and wild sea spray, Carina and Henry caught sight of the *Essex* captain. *Of course, it would be Lieutenant Scarfield,* Carina thought, recognizing the soldier and his fiendish smile. He ordered his crew to light the ship cannons—all thirty of them.

"He's going to blast us out of the water!" Carina shouted to Henry with alarm. "What do we do?"

Suddenly, another shape loomed behind the *Essex*. A shadow straight from the depths of hell . . .

The *Silent Mary* had finally caught up. It rose, opening its massive hull like a giant mouth.

Carina watched in horror as the ghost ship descended upon the *Essex*, snapping the warship in two. In a blazing fireball, the *Essex* exploded from within, all the gunpowder aboard igniting at once. Carina felt the heat graze her skin as the *Essex* was completely consumed.

The crew aboard the *Black Pearl* gaped at the wreckage. But the *Silent Mary* didn't even pause. It continued to cut through the sea as though nothing had been in its way.

Barbossa moved toward Carina. "Whatever happens, stay your course," he instructed her.

Instantly, everyone aboard the *Black Pearl* ran to battle stations, and Henry rushed over to help. Men loaded cannons and rifles. Swords were thrown to crewmates with abandon.

Barbossa's men were loyal to the end; they were not going down without a fight.

There was no escape; the *Silent Mary* drew up alongside the *Pearl*, its prey finally at hand.

Captain Salazar jumped onto the deck of the *Black Pearl*,

hanger sword in hand. His wicked delight was clear.

"We've come with the butcher's bill!" he cried savagely.

With a horrible roar, all the ghost pirates boarded the *Black Pearl*, ready to kill.

Swords clashed and screams echoed behind Carina as she desperately steered the ship along their course.

"Where is Jack Sparrow?" she heard Salazar cry with contempt as the battle raged on. *"Where is he?"*

Salazar caught sight of Jack's ropes piled in a heap by the mast he'd been tied to. He howled, "There is nowhere to hide!"

Suddenly, the *Pearl* hit a precariously pitched wave and dipped. Men screamed as ghost pirates descended upon them. They battled for their lives, but the dead were proving too much of a match.

Out of the corner of her eye, Carina caught a glimpse of Henry throwing a long rope to Jack, and Jack's shadowy figure swinging across to the *Silent Mary*. The pirate had boarded the ghost ship.

Salazar stared furiously at his target. "Leave him to me."

With a running leap, Salazar threw himself across the watery chasm separating the ships and landed on a cannon beside Jack aboard the *Silent Mary*. Both men drew their swords and began fighting.

"I will break you this time!" Salazar seethed, punctuating his sentence with a clash of his sword.

"Punish you for the pain I must endure!"

CLANK!

"Feeling my own death over and over!"

CLANK! CLANK!

"Or you could simply forgive me," Jack pointed out, leaping back to stand on the *Pearl*.

While the two men were locked in battle, Carina heard the brutal sounds of combat raging behind her aboard the *Pearl*. Yet she remained loyal to her word. She never let go of the wheel; she steered them true among the wind and pain and carnage.

Captain Barbossa stayed by her side, desperately fighting off ghost pirates left and right to keep her safe while she held her eyes on the stars.

Suddenly, Barbossa slipped, and his leg caught in the boards of the ship deck. A ghost howled with unearthly laughter as he slashed the captain's side. Barbossa groaned, injured.

Another ghost descended on him, ready to run the old man through. Carina realized that without help, Barbossa was finished.

Thinking fast, she swung herself around the ship wheel, kicking Barbossa's trapped leg free. The old pirate captain rolled to the side and clashed with the ghost, fending him off just in time. Barbossa's eyes flashed thanks to Carina before he began battling again, keeping the dead at bay.

Meanwhile, Salazar continued to scream at Jack.

"You took everything from me! Made me more repulsive than any pirate!"

The men were dueling on the deck of the *Silent Mary*, sparks flying between their swords.

"That's not necessarily true," Jack pointed out. "Have you met Edward the Blue? He's very repulsive."

Suddenly, a grotesque groan echoed from the bow of the *Silent Mary*. Jack watched with horror as the carved female figurehead from the front of the ship detached herself and began crawling toward him.

"That's very strange," Jack said. "But I like your dress."

The figurehead let out a horrifying scream as she bore down on Jack. And now he was fighting off two devilish spirits side by side. Jack was trapped aboard the *Silent Mary* with death surrounding him and nowhere to run. He was finished.

But not if Carina had anything to say about it. Armed with anger and frustration at having witnessed yet another impossible occurrence, Carina made some quick calculations in her head. Then, with a mighty heave, she sent the *Black Pearl* barreling into the side of the *Silent Mary*, the two ships crashing together with titanic impact, all the while still sailing straight on course.

The gruesome female figurehead was crushed and Jack was flung to the deck of the *Pearl*, snatched from the jaws of death.

"Carina!" Henry cried out as he made his way to her right. He was battered and bleeding, drained with exhaustion.

At her left, Barbossa bled heavily from the wound in his side. He couldn't hold the ghosts off much longer.

And at the edge of the ship, Salazar had cornered Jack once more. Hell's fury burned in the captain's eyes as he prepared to send Jack to his demise.

With dread, Carina realized that her maneuver hadn't had the impact she had hoped; they were losing. She looked up, desperately trying to find some sort of clue in the sky. But the sun was starting to rise, making the stars disappear.

"It's almost daylight!" she cried. "I'm running out of time. The stars will soon be gone."

Just because you can't see something doesn't mean it's not there. The familiar words ran across her mind.

And then she saw it.

"Henry, look!"

Dawn broke, revealing a massive black rock island splitting the sea.

"The X in the middle of the sea!" Carina cried. It was an island after all.

Henry's eyes grew wide. "You found it!"

Likewise, all the ghost pirates' eyes grew wide—with fear.

"*Land!*" they cried. "*Get to the Mary!*"

The ghosts desperately retreated to the back of the *Pearl*, fleeing for their undead souls.

And Carina knew what she had to do.

With a final burst of effort, she sailed the *Black Pearl* straight onto the island, beaching the entire ship.

The ghosts unlucky enough to still be at the front screamed as they disintegrated.

"Nooo!" Salazar howled, his sword mere inches from Jack's throat. He was prevented from reaching his target by the invisible barrier created by the rock.

Desperate with wrath, Salazar had no choice but to back away—but not before reaching out to grab Carina from the wheel. . . .

"Carina!"

In a blur, Henry stepped between her and Salazar, allowing the ghost captain to capture him instead. Carina reached wildly for Henry, but it was too late. Salazar dragged the boy back with him aboard the *Silent Mary*, and the ghost ship veered away from the land, taking Henry along with it.

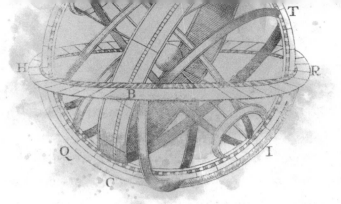

CHAPTER 32

"HENRY!" CARINA SCREAMED. "We have to go back for Henry!"

Barbossa stepped up beside her, holding his bleeding side. "The Trident is the only thing that can save him now," he said. "We must find it, before it is too late."

Desperation burned inside Carina. Henry couldn't be captured—not now, not when they were so close to achieving their goal.

I don't want to lose him, she realized, feeling the full weight of how much he meant to her.

But the logical part of her mind knew Barbossa was right.

They couldn't defeat the dead—not without the Trident. It was the only thing that could bring Henry back to her.

I'll save you, Henry, Carina thought. *I promise.*

Together, Jack, Carina, and Barbossa looked down over the rail at the strange black island. It was unlike any land Carina had ever seen before: a deserted beach carved out of volcanic rock. Steam rose from it, giving it the appearance of a distant planet.

"It's empty, but this has to be it," Carina said.

Suddenly, the light of the rising sun reflected off millions of tiny specks covering the surface of the black island.

"Those are diamonds," a pirate breathed.

The crew members looked at one another.

"We're rich!" they cried.

Instantly, several pirates leaped down to the island. One of them tugged eagerly at a twinkling stone embedded in the rock.

FWOOM!

A blast of hot steam burst up from a crack in the rock. The crack grew larger and larger until it became a deep chasm. The pirate who had reached for the diamond was suddenly sucked down into it.

The other pirates stared at the empty space where he had been.

"Back to the ship!" they cried.

They all fled for their lives. But Carina stepped forward.

The sun rose higher, reflecting more and more diamonds on the surface of the rock. They shimmered and shone, twinkling brighter than any other gems in existence. Carina instantly recognized the picture they painted.

"Look at it, Jack," Carina breathed. "It is the most beautiful thing I've ever seen."

"Yes, beautiful rocks," Jack said uncertainly. "That kill for no reason."

"Not rocks, Jack," Carina said. "Stars."

Carina climbed down from the ship, and Jack and Barbossa followed close behind.

"Did you say *stars*?" Jack asked.

"Stars and planets exactly as they appear in the sky." Carina nodded, amazed. "This island is a perfect reflection of the heavens."

Carina walked forward more quickly. Jack chased after her.

"But they're still rocks!" he insisted. "Murderous rocks!"

"Something's missing," Carina said, focused. "The X in the sky. The Southern Cross."

She stepped lightly across the island, walking amid a sea of stars against a black backdrop. To anyone watching, it would have seemed the girl was walking across the sky.

She searched and searched, knowing it must be there.

And then she saw the cluster of stars from Galileo's diary. Here the constellation was made up of sparkling *rubies* instead of diamonds embedded in the rock. They glowed crimson under the sun. But the star in the middle—the crux of the Southern Cross—seemed different from the others. It was dull and did not glow like the rest of the gems.

Barbossa drew up alongside Carina and handed her the ruby from Galileo's diary.

"Finish it, Carina," he said.

Carina took the ruby, feeling its full weight in her hand.

"For my father," she said.

Barbossa stared at her for a long moment. "Aye, for your father."

Carina removed the dull rock from the ground and set her ruby in the space among the five stars—a perfect fit, like a key fitting into a lock

The sunlight reflected off the ruby like never before, and it started to glow like the others. Then, one by one, the other stars in the constellation lit up, forming the shape of the Trident in a brilliant red display.

"X marks the spot!" she cried.

The rumble was faint at first, a deep hum within the island. But it grew louder and louder, and the sea in front of them began to shift. Jack grabbed Carina just as a deep crack opened beneath her feet, shooting up steam, separating them from Barbossa. The island quaked violently, and the ocean swirled as though an invisible force was disturbing it. Barbossa had no choice but to head back to the ship with his men.

It's splitting, Carina realized, watching the water intently as the world rocked around her.

Before their very eyes, an invisible wind tore the ocean apart, creating two unfathomable walls of water hundreds of feet high, slowly exposing the bottom of the sea.

Then the floor beneath them shook, propelling Carina and Jack down the watery chasm toward the ocean floor itself. They knew the treasure—the thing they had risked so much to find—was waiting at the bottom.

It was time to find the Trident of Poseidon.

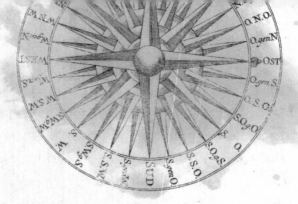

CHAPTER 33

THE BOTTOM OF THE SEA WAS INCREDIBLE. ALL her life Carina had been looking to the sky. How could she ever have thought, ever have known, that all her searching would bring her to that destination: the floor of the ocean, between two mountainous walls of water?

Shadows of sea creatures swam in and out of view behind the curtains of water. An invisible force kept the ocean at bay, though the water thundered on both sides of Jack and Carina.

"How far do you think we need to go?" Carina asked.

"Apparently, not far at all." Jack pointed ahead.

Carina looked and gasped.

Before them, the chasm grew even wider, opening to reveal a temple made out of coral. And in the center, on a pedestal of craggy sea rock, stood the treasure.

"The Trident," Carina breathed.

She could barely believe it. After a lifetime of studying and searching and hoping . . . there it was. The key to Carina's birthright. The key to saving Henry. The key to everything!

Carina raced forward, holding up her dress as she drew closer to the curved, jutting rocks.

"Jack!"

Carina turned toward the familiar voice and gasped. Henry was rushing toward them.

"Henry!" she cried. But he pushed her aside, taking out his sword and swinging it at Jack. Jack dodged the blade at the last minute, and the two of them squared off as Carina got to her feet.

The pirate peered at Henry while they circled each other. "Arms straight, shoulders square, front legs bent . . ."

"*Henry?*" Carina stared at him in shock as Jack voiced what she was thinking.

"Pretty sure that's not Henry."

Henry went for the pirate again, his eyes filled with an unearthly rage. It seemed that Salazar had somehow found a way to walk on land—through Henry.

Thinking quickly, Carina rushed toward the pedestal

holding the Trident. She grabbed hold of the mythical arti-
fact, struggling to free it from its rocky throne. Finally, it
gave, almost knocking Carina off balance with its sheer size
and weight.

She pivoted, pointing the Trident toward the possessed
Henry. He had backed Jack into the curtains of water. The
cracked, pale arms of Salazar's ghost men reached for Jack
through the sea.

"Leave him," Carina commanded Henry. "Drop your
sword!" She wielded the Trident like a weapon.

Henry walked slowly toward Carina, his undivided attention now on her.

"Carina . . ." Jack said hesitantly.

"Henry, please . . ." Carina searched Henry's gleaming
eyes as he approached. She desperately tried to get through
to the part of him that was still the caring young man who
seemed to understand her. The young man on a quest to
save his father. The young man who had taught her that just
because you couldn't see something didn't mean it wasn't
there.

Soon he was right in front of her. Carina hesitated, and
Henry knocked the Trident away from her, grabbing the
ancient weapon.

"It's over, Jack!" he announced sinisterly, lifting the
Trident over his head. The ocean floor began to shake, and
the water pulled apart even farther, flowing straight up.

And then the ghost of Captain Salazar emerged, casting Henry's body to the ground. The dead sea captain grinned savagely, his eyes shining with vicious confidence. It was Salazar unlike they'd ever seen him before: commanding, supreme, and thirsty for blood. He held the Trident out as water circled him.

Carina rushed to Henry's side. She took his head in her hands and felt his neck for a pulse. She gasped in relief. He was breathing.

Meanwhile, Salazar was making his way to Jack.

"*Hola*, Sparrow," Salazar sneered. Using the Trident's power, he flung Jack up against a craggy sea rock with invisible force.

"Henry, wake up!" Carina cried, shaking him.

But Henry didn't stir.

Thwomp! Salazar continued to use the Trident's power to fling Jack around like a rag doll. *Thwomp! Thwomp! Thwomp!*

With each impact, Carina could have sworn she heard Jack's bones breaking.

She reached out to grab water from the sea wall to splash on Henry's face. Salazar's ghost crew taunted Carina, jeering at her through the water. She had forgotten they were there, waiting for their curse to be broken so they could accompany their captain.

"Oh, bugger off," she snapped. She did not have time for their supernatural antics. Without hesitating, she scooped a handful of water from the wall and doused Henry. "Henry, wake up! He's killing Jack!"

Henry's eyes fluttered open. He groaned, dazed and unfocused.

"Salazar can walk on land with the Trident," Carina whispered urgently.

Meanwhile, Jack continued to flail helplessly as Salazar smashed him back and forth, in and out of the water, up against stone and coral and earth.

"The power of the sea," Henry murmured, finally coming to.

Carina recited the words from the diary: "'To release the power of the sea, all must divide.'"

"Divide?" Henry asked.

Jack landed in a heap at the base of the massive coral temple. Salazar stepped forward, victory gleaming in his eyes. He brandished the Trident, holding the power of a god, ready to claim his revenge once and for all.

"If the Trident holds all the power . . ." Carina started.

"Then every curse is held inside," Henry realized.

Carina's eyes widened. That was it!

"All must divide, Henry!" she cried.

"Divide, divide," Henry replied. Understanding flashed across his face. "Break!"

Jack stumbled to his feet, staring death in the face.

"Surrender to me now, and I'll let you live," he slurred, half-conscious, to Salazar.

Salazar laughed. "You want me to surrender?"

"I highly recommend it," said Jack.

Salazar's eyes blazed with hatred. "This is where the tale ends!"

With cataclysmic force, Salazar plunged the Trident straight into Jack's chest, close to his heart. Henry and Carina watched in horror. Henry stumbled to his feet.

"No!" screamed Carina.

"Shhh," Salazar whispered, eyes on Jack. He held one end of the Trident while Jack clung to the prongs piercing his chest. "Jack Sparrow is no more."

But for some reason, despite the blood that was spreading across his chest, Jack grinned.

He opened his shirt wide, revealing Galileo's diary. He had used it as a shield, preventing the wounds from being life-threatening. For a split second Carina wondered when he had taken the diary. But then something else distracted her.

Glowing on the front of the book were the words Carina had discovered in the light of the blood moon.

TO RELEASE THE POWER OF THE SEA, ALL MUST DIVIDE.

"Henry!" Jack hollered.

Henry's face was set, determined. "Carina, I have to break it!" he said. "If I break the Trident, I'll break every curse at sea!"

225

She nodded, knowing it was the only thing they could do. With a surge of newfound energy, Henry charged forward.

Meanwhile, Jack used all his strength to keep Salazar from removing the Trident from his chest. But the ghost captain was unrelenting.

"Adios," Salazar spat.

He never even saw Henry coming, sword held high, ready to right a thousand wrongs.

CRASH!

In a blast of light, Henry brought his sword down on the Trident, splitting it in two.

A ripple emanated from the broken Trident like an aftershock, roiling the very fabric of the ocean itself.

"Nooo!" Salazar screamed in fury. He looked down at his hands and dropped his half of the Trident on the ocean floor.

Salazar's men began tumbling out from the curtains of water, sputtering and coughing.

Carina stared at them in awe. Their wounds had been healed, their eyes clear once more.

Salazar reached up to feel the back of his head. It was whole again.

For a single confused, terrifying moment, everything stood still.

Their curse had been lifted; they lived once again.

Then the sea rumbled.

Streams began to shoot out from the walls of water on

both sides of the cavern as if through cracks in a glass tank under too much pressure.

"It's collapsing!" yelled Carina.

Jack and Henry ran up alongside her.

"We have to run!"

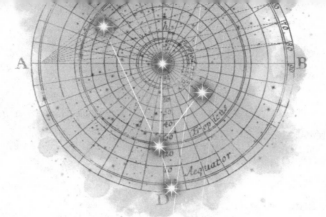

Chapter 34

BENEATH WHERE THE *BLACK PEARL* FLOATED AT the rim of the parted ocean, Barbossa waited, hanging from an anchor. He and the others had dropped it to the floor of the sea, awaiting Jack and Carina's return.

"Hurry!" Barbossa cried as the trio sprinted into view.

Not far behind them were Salazar and his crew.

Jack, Carina, and Henry dove for the anchor and began climbing as the sea collapsed around them. The swirling ocean churned, trying to suck them down. Some of Salazar's men screamed, disappearing beneath the waves. Carina, Jack, and Henry climbed up, up, up, with Salazar and his men hot on their heels.

The men on board the *Black Pearl* tried to help by pulling up the anchor, but it was too heavy with the weight of so many people. The ship tipped, dipping the anchor lower.

The motion knocked everyone off balance. Carina slipped!

"I've got you!" Barbossa cried, reaching down to grab her hand.

He caught hold of Carina just before the force from the racing water would have dragged her back down. She dangled above the sea floor, Salazar's men moving up fast behind them.

"Come on!" Henry urged them from above.

Carina scrambled back onto the rope and clung to it tightly when she spotted something odd. Something *impossible* . . .

Tattooed on Barbossa's arm was a cluster of five stars—the same five stars from Galileo's diary.

The same five stars that had guided her whole life.

Carina gazed at Hector Barbossa, seeing him clearly for the first time. For a moment, the thundering noise of the waves and the cries of men's voices grew muffled, distant. Time seemed to stand still. Carina locked eyes with Barbossa, feeling her heart break in a way she didn't know possible.

This old man from the islands was suddenly so real. More than a diary, more than a birthright. A worn, weathered sea captain, who nineteen years earlier had hobbled up to a children's home with a basket, a baby, and a book.

"What am I to you?" Carina asked Barbossa.

Salazar was just feet behind her, dagger in hand, ready to strike.

And yet Barbossa smiled.

"Treasure," he answered.

From above, Jack dropped his sword. In one smooth motion, Barbossa caught it—and let go of the rope.

He dropped on top of Salazar, plunging the sword deep into the now living captain's heart. Salazar screamed while Barbossa continued to fall, his sword taking out more of Salazar's men as he went.

Carina watched in disbelief, tears in her eyes as Barbossa disappeared beneath the swirling water, lost to the collapsing wall of waves. But she could have sworn that before he vanished, he smiled at her—at peace.

As quickly as she had come to know Barbossa as her father, he was gone. And the sea was closing upon them. There was no time to grieve—only time to climb.

"Hang on!" cried Henry.

The men aboard the *Black Pearl* put everything they had into hauling up the anchor as the sea swelled around Jack, Carina, and Henry. They climbed with all their strength, the roaring ocean swelling up around them . . .

And they broke through the surface just as the walls collapsed completely!

A moment later, the ocean was restored. The *Black Pearl* righted itself with a mighty splash.

Jack, Carina, and Henry dropped to the deck, coughing and sputtering. Darkness lifted from the ocean, revealing a perfect, calm sea.

Jack walked to the rail as sun sliced through the clouds. The crew joined him, and they all removed their hats in a moment of respect for their lost captain.

"A pirate's life, Hector," Jack said.

Henry helped a shaky Carina to her feet.

"Are you okay?" he asked.

Carina felt inexplicable emotions welling up inside her. A life of questions finally answered—but at what cost?

"For a moment, I had everything," she whispered, "only to lose it all again."

Henry handed her the diary that had always meant so much to her, and then held her close. "Not everything, Ms. Smyth," he said.

At that, Carina smiled through her tears. "Barbossa," she said, embracing Henry so tightly it felt like she might never let go. "My name is Barbossa."

CHAPTER 35

A FEW DAYS LATER, Carina and Henry stood at the edge of a cluster of island cliffs, gazing out at the calm sea.

"Do you think it worked?" Carina asked Henry. "Do you think your father's curse has been broken?"

Henry looked down at a small piece of the Trident Jack had left him after their adventure. "I don't know," he admitted. "But if it did, then this is where he'll be. This is the one place he always swore to come back to."

Carina took Henry's hand. All her life she had felt alone. But not anymore. She now knew the truth of who she was and where she'd come from. And yet, in seeking her birthright, she'd discovered something completely different: a companion on the same quest—two hearts so similar they couldn't help joining after such an adventure.

"Then I am glad to be with you here, Henry Turner," she said.

Henry smiled. "Maybe Jack was right."

"About what?" asked Carina.

"About you and me," Henry replied.

Very slowly, Henry leaned down to kiss Carina . . .

And she slapped him in the face.

"What are you doing?" Henry asked, stung.

"Just making sure it's truly you," Carina replied.

"It's me!" Henry insisted. "It's still me!"

"Then I guess I was . . ." Carina started.

"Wrong!" exclaimed Henry, grinning. "The word is *wrong*."

"Slightly in error." Carina smiled back. "Although, one could argue—"

With that, Henry did kiss her. Carina held him close, feeling as though her heart might burst.

When they finally parted, Henry gazed tenderly at Carina and brushed back her hair.

"Apology accepted," he said.

Suddenly, something on the sea horizon caught his eye.

"Do you see that?" he asked Carina excitedly.

She and Henry looked through a spyglass to see a ship coming toward the shore.

"The *Dutchman*!" Henry breathed. "My father's ship!"

Henry and Carina raced across the cliffs when the ship arrived. A man climbed up the rocky shore—Will Turner. He was tall and handsome, bearing a striking resemblance to Henry, Carina thought.

But he had the older, wiser, loving look of a father.

"Let me look at you, Son," Will said.

Henry threw his arms around his father, and the two embraced for a long while. Carina watched happily, letting her tears fall freely. Father and son were reunited. Henry and Carina had both found their fathers, really.

"How did you do it, Henry?" Will asked in disbelief. He looked from Henry to Carina. "How did you save me?"

Henry took Carina's hand, beaming. "Let me tell you a story," he said, "a tale of the greatest treasure any man can hold."

Will placed his arms around Carina and Henry. "That's a tale I'd like to hear."

Carina beamed, too. She looked up to the sky, knowing that even though she couldn't see it, the star was there. Her star. The star that had finally, after so many years, guided her home.

The brightest star in the north.